# Falling Under You

# Also from Laurelin Paige

**The Fixed Trilogy**
Fixed on You
Found in You
Forever with You
Hudson
Falling Under You: A Fixed Trilogy Novella (1001 Dark Nights)
Chandler—Coming Fall 2016

**Found Duet**
Free Me
Find Me

**Lights, Camera**
Take Two
Star Struck

**First Touch**
Last Kiss —Coming Summer 2016

*Co-Written Works:*
Written with Sierra Simone:
Porn Star

Written with Kayti McGee:
Miss Match
Love Struck
MisTaken: A Novella
Screwmates—Coming Fall 2016

# Falling Under You

## A Fixed Trilogy Novella

## By Laurelin Paige

1001 Dark Nights

EVIL EYE

CONCEPTS

Falling Under You
A Fixed Trilogy Novella
By Laurelin Paige

1001 Dark Nights
Copyright 2016 Laurelin Paige
ISBN: 978-1-940887-96-8

Foreword: Copyright 2014 M. J. Rose
Published by Evil Eye Concepts, Incorporated

This is a work of fiction. Names, places, characters and incidents are the product of the author's imagination and are fictitious. Any resemblance to actual persons, living or dead, events or establishments is solely coincidental.

# Acknowledgments

To my husband and kids—Thank you for knowing how to love the Norma Anders that I am. It's a true blessing.

To Liz Berry, Jillian Stein, and MJ Rose—You are an absolute treasure in the world of romance. I'm so lucky to have met you and even more lucky to be included in your circle of friendship.

To my "people", Rebecca Friedman, Jenn Watson, Ashley Lindemann, Sheri Gustafson, Melissa Gaston, Sierra Simone, Kayti McGee, and Melanie Harlow—Best. Squad. Ever.

To my Fixed Trilogy readers—There aren't words for how much I appreciate the love you've given these characters. It's truly humbling and astounding. Thank you!!

To my God—Always, I remain fixed on you.

Sign up for the 1001 Dark Nights Newsletter
and be entered to win a Tiffany Key necklace.

There's a contest every month!

Go to www.1001DarkNights.com to subscribe.

As a bonus, all subscribers will receive a free
1001 Dark Nights story
The First Night
by Lexi Blake & M.J. Rose

# One Thousand and One Dark Nights

*Once upon a time, in the future…*

*I was a student fascinated with stories and learning.
I studied philosophy, poetry, history, the occult, and
the art and science of love and magic. I had a vast
library at my father's home and collected thousands
of volumes of fantastic tales.*

*I learned all about ancient races and bygone
times. About myths and legends and dreams of all
people through the millennium. And the more I read
the stronger my imagination grew until I discovered
that I was able to travel into the stories... to actually
become part of them.*

*I wish I could say that I listened to my teacher
and respected my gift, as I ought to have. If I had, I
would not be telling you this tale now.
But I was foolhardy and confused, showing off
with bravery.*

*One afternoon, curious about the myth of the
Arabian Nights, I traveled back to ancient Persia to
see for myself if it was true that every day Shahryar
(Persian: شهریار, "king") married a new virgin, and then
sent yesterday's wife to be beheaded. It was written
and I had read, that by the time he met Scheherazade,
the vizier's daughter, he'd killed one thousand
women.*

*Something went wrong with my efforts. I arrived
in the midst of the story and somehow exchanged
places with Scheherazade – a phenomena that had
never occurred before and that still to this day, I
cannot explain.*

*Now I am trapped in that ancient past. I have
taken on Scheherazade's life and the only way I can
protect myself and stay alive is to do what she did to
protect herself and stay alive.*

*Every night the King calls for me and listens as I spin tales.
And when the evening ends and dawn breaks, I stop at a
point that leaves him breathless and yearning for more.
And so the King spares my life for one more day, so that
he might hear the rest of my dark tale.*

*As soon as I finish a story... I begin a new
one... like the one that you, dear reader, have before
you now.*

# Chapter One

*July*

I pushed the door open and stepped onto the rooftop, grateful for the empty landscape if not for the hot, muggy night. *Escape.* That's what this was. A much-needed escape.

I walked over to the railing and looked down at the street below, but my attention was still on the scene I'd just left. The awkward, horribly embarrassing scene. I groaned out loud. I could still see the look on Hudson's face when I'd cornered him in the hallway and kissed him. Could still hear the disdain in his voice as he'd pushed me away and said, *"You don't want what I have to give, Norma. Trust me."*

But I *did* want what he had to give. At least, I was pretty sure I did. After the disappointing series of men I'd dated who'd failed to satisfy me in the bedroom, I'd realized I craved a lover with the confident, powerful strength of a man like Hudson Pierce. A man who controlled and had authority over me in every way possible. I'd thought that he would be the one guy who could handle that I was a smart, successful woman without letting it intimidate him. As his chief financial advisor, I'd been his right hand "man" for years. Couldn't I also be the perfect companion elsewhere? The potential of the power couple we could make was scary and thrilling all at once.

Apparently, he didn't have the same vision.

My flaws ran through my mind like bullet points on a PowerPoint presentation.

Too old (thirty-four, which was only a digit off from thirty-five)

Too serious (how else did a woman get to where I was in the business world?)

Too independent (I didn't depend on anyone for anything, though I'd prefer the real deal to my seven-inch battery-operated boyfriend)

Too…not blond (the most frequent hair color of the women I'd seen on Hudson's arm)

I groaned again. *Stupid, stupid, stupid.* What the hell had I been thinking? Obviously, I hadn't been. I couldn't even blame my behavior on being drunk—though there was plenty of alcohol at the event downstairs, I'd touched nothing but water all evening. The party was meant to be a celebration. Pierce Industries had just closed its highest earning year ever, and I was a key player in that success. Silly me for thinking that a better way to celebrate would be to announce my infatuation with my boss instead of raising a toast like everyone else.

God, Monday was going to suck. How could I face Hudson without turning beet red with shame ever again?

The roof door slammed shut behind me. Startled, I turned in that direction, letting out my breath when I saw it was my assistant, Boyd. He approached the railing, and I scanned him over as he did, an action that almost caused me to sigh again. As sure as I was that I could be in love with Hudson Pierce, I was in most definite lust with Boyd Barrett. His suit was perfectly tailored to highlight his trim hips and toned upper body. And the way his hair flopped over his eyes, as though he didn't give a shit about looking put together, yet pulling that messy look off with a precision that suggested he'd worked for it…yeah, he was truly a work of art.

He was a good assistant too. In the year he'd worked for me, he'd proven himself as the best employee I'd ever had, and not only because he was so delightful to look at.

Jesus, I really needed to get laid. Between my boss and my subordinate, I was halfway to getting charged with sexual harassment.

But I'd never make a move on Boyd. He was *my* right-hand man, even at only twenty-six years of age—a detail often overshadowed by his skills and competence. A detail that I remembered again when I truly took a moment to gaze at the smooth baby face—which he usually hid behind a pair of nerdy, dark glasses—and his young, fit body. He probably had a six-pack tucked under those layers of clothes. *I bet he could go for hours...*

Suddenly feeling warm, I turned to look back over the city below me before my thoughts got too dirty. "You found the fortress of solitude." I hoped my voice didn't betray my naughty fantasizing. "Unless you were looking for me?" I added, realizing he might need a signature or a directive. Even though it was a Friday night, it wouldn't have surprised me to find Boyd was still on the clock. He was as much of a workaholic as I was.

He lifted his foot and braced it on the lowest rail. "I was, as a matter of fact. I noticed you slip out and wanted to make sure you were okay."

Ugh. How was I supposed to answer that? I felt like shit, but I was okay. I was *always* okay. That was me—strong, enduring. Even when I had egg on my face. Even when I was forced to admit that hooking up with my crush was never going to happen.

Not that I'd say any of that to my employee. Putting on a tight smile, I dismissed his concern. "I'm fine."

"That's a lie. You're not fine."

Boyd's uncharacteristically brash response caught me by surprise. I turned my head toward him, my brow raised, my mouth open to correct his impudence.

But he spoke first, his tone rumbling with authority. "I'll only ask once more, Norma, and this time I expect an answer—what's wrong?"

The depth of the demand, the way his blue eyes seared into me, the dark, sensual way he spoke my name (a name he never used, a name I usually hated)—all of it was fuel to a fire I hadn't realized this boy could kindle.

Strike that—this *man*.

Warmth rippled down my spine and spread to my center, awakening my senses, stirring my arousal, weakening my knees. And Norma Anders rarely got weak knees. I'd never seen this side of Boyd. I'd barely ever seen this side of *me*, and goddammit, I liked it.

He was still waiting for my answer, his gaze patient and

demanding all at once, and while I should have been formulating a response that would cut the power to the strange energy field that suddenly encircled us, all I could think about was how hypnotic his eyes were, wondering if he was wearing contacts or if his work glasses were just for show.

So when I spoke, I wasn't thinking—I was reacting. "I made a pass at someone." The words tumbled past my lips, as though compelled simply by Boyd's command. "A stupid, foolish pass. It wasn't reciprocated."

Boyd's eye ticked, probably annoyed that he'd gone to so much trouble to elicit a confession that boiled down to, "*I got hurt by a boy.*" Even I recognized the pettiness.

Except, it didn't feel petty. It stung and I hated how much. I particularly hated how weak it made me appear, and I gave into the urge to validate my emotions. "It wasn't a pass I made lightly. I've thought about it for a long time, and logically, it seemed like it was the natural progression of our relationship."

Maybe it was the tilt of Boyd's head or the purse of his lips, or maybe I'd simply opened the floodgates by voicing feelings that I'd kept stowed away, but I wanted to tell him more, words that had no motivation except the desire to be spoken. "I don't know how he couldn't have noticed me. I'm here, every day, right in front of him. Yet he's never batted an eye in my direction that doesn't have to do with business. Can you imagine how that feels? To be praised and admired for my work ethic but never acknowledged as an attractive member of the opposite sex? To plug away, side by side, for years and never catch even one flirtatious glance? Do you know what that's like?"

I threw my head back, pissed at myself for the eruption of emotion, willing my assistant to ignore what I'd said and go away instead of attempting to console me.

He *didn't* try to console me. Instead, without missing a beat, he answered my hypothetical question earnestly. "Yes, actually, I do know what that's like."

My breath caught, understanding instantly whom he was talking about. There was only one person he worked alongside, and before his current position, he'd been in graduate school.

For the second time that night, my knees felt ready to give out.

Something fluttered in my belly that I wanted to dismiss but couldn't.

Carefully—cautiously—I twisted my head back toward Boyd. I had no comeback. No words as I studied the strong sweep of his jaw, the intent tilt of his chin. Boyd had feelings for *me*? It wasn't something I'd ever seriously considered. Sure I liked to imagine what he looked like naked, but that was feelings-free. I was eight years his senior. I was his boss. It wasn't smart to fancy a coworker, especially when the company emphatically disallowed fraternization between management and subordinates.

Oh. Wait.

Hudson could very well have had similar thoughts about me.

And I'd been hurt by his brush-off, which was reason enough for me to hear Boyd out.

But also, more enticing even, I wanted to hear more because of how his revelation made me feel. Unsteady and nervous and turned on.

It was a bad idea, though. A wickedly delicious bad idea.

Boyd interrupted my internal debate. "You're thinking too much."

My lungs felt pressed as I tried to keep an even tone to my response. "That's what I do."

"Right now you need to stop thinking and listen." Again, his voice was weighted with a dominance that I had to obey.

"Okay."

He bored his gaze further into me. "Hudson Pierce is not the man for you."

My mouth gaped. I'd never said I was talking about Hudson. I worked with a predominately male staff—had I been more obvious than I'd thought?

Boyd didn't give me time to dwell. "You're attracted to him because there's a part of your life that needs a strong, controlling man, but a man like him would never let you be the equally strong, independent woman that you are. He would always try to top you in your career and your relationships with others and you would always be unfulfilled."

His words were tiny pins, their truth pricking at the bubble of a fantasy I'd created about my employer and myself. I tried to hold the air in, covering the holes. "But maybe that's what I need."

"It *is* what you need." His raw conviction made me dizzy. "But only in well-defined areas."

"Such as?"

"The bedroom." He hadn't moved closer, yet there suddenly seemed to be no space between us, and the air crackled with an energy that shot hot lasers to the skin inside my thighs. "There you need a man who will bring you to your knees."

"That's very"—*accurate*—"vague." My heart thudded like a drum in my ears, a thousand beats seeming to fill each second of time.

He chuckled, a sound that itched at my desire like sandpaper. "Imagine this then. Imagine a man who never interferes with your business decisions. He stands by them. He takes your advice and direction readily. He admires the way that you take care of your siblings and everyone else around you. The way you keep everything in order and structured.

"Then you bring him here, to this company party. After you've fulfilled your obligations and you're ready, when you give the signal, he takes over."

"Takes over how?" My voice was so breathy that my words came out as no more than a whisper.

He lifted a finger up to shush me, landing millimeters in front of my mouth without actually touching it. "I'm getting there."

It took every ounce of strength not to press closer, not to let my lips brush across his skin.

His eyes twinkled as though recognizing and delighting in my struggle. He dropped his hand—I swear it was meant to torture me—and leaned against the railing with the panache of a man twice his age. "He tells you to make your way to conference room B. You'll leave the light off, but the blinds will stay open so that you can see well enough from the moon. There you'll take off your panties and your stockings and lay them neatly over the chair. You'll put your shoes back on and roll the chair out of the way. Then you'll bend over the table, your arms stretched out in front of you, palms facedown, your ass up in the air. And you'll wait."

Each word scraped at my decorum, perking my lust like the ears of a dog when he sees the chains of his leash and knows he's about to be walked.

"What if someone came in?" But my subtext was, *what do I have to do to get on the other end of that leash?*

"That wouldn't be your concern." Boyd practically *ts*ked in his chiding. "You'd let him worry about that. You wouldn't question him either. Once you gave the signal, you'd give him the power. He'd give the orders, no arguments, no hesitation."

I'd never had a lover that took charge. As in every other area of my life, I gravitated toward the alpha role and the men I'd dated fell contently into the opposing position. It wasn't what I'd wanted—it was just how it was. It was just what men did.

But what if one man didn't? I wondered if the lilt in my voice betrayed how often I daydreamed about exactly this type of scenario when I asked, "What would happen then?"

Boyd's eyes narrowed, studying me, his gaze lingering so long on my lips I thought he might be considering kissing me.

Finally he said, "What happens next would be better shown than told."

I straightened, putting distance between us. We'd suddenly moved from fantasy to possibility and were quickly skating toward probability. I was clearheaded enough to recognize that as inappropriate. This entire conversation was inappropriate. And dangerous.

It was also intoxicating. Boyd seemed to know things about me that I'd only just begun to realize about myself. Things I needed desperately to explore.

Still, I could be responsible. I had to be. "There are too many reasons why that would be a bad idea." Enough said. Case closed.

"Yes, there are," he agreed. "Forget them." The last sentence was a command.

I fought against the order, wanting what he was suggesting with acute desire. "I'm not sure I'm the kind of person who can."

"You can." He leaned in over my shoulder, his breath skating across the skin of my neck. "You just haven't encountered the kind of guy who can help you do it."

I shivered from the heat of his insinuation. "And you think you're that guy?"

"I know that I am." He moved his mouth along my jawline, never touching me with anything but the hot air that passed between his lips. "Let me show you who I am. Let me show you who *you* are."

# Chapter Two

The latest glance at my wristwatch said I'd been waiting for Boyd for twelve minutes. Stretching my arms out on the conference table in front of me had felt good at first, but it was unnatural, and holding the position was becoming difficult mentally, if not actually physically. Twelve minutes was a lot of time to think through the situation. The list of pros and cons had been thoroughly culled, and it was more accurate to call it simply a list of cons.

Against company policy to mix management levels

An eight-year age gap between us

Nearly impossible to continue working with someone you'd screwed

This was Boyd! The sweet kid who filtered through my calls and e-mails and got me coffee! How good could the sex be?

Fooling around on office premises was a horrible idea

The last item on the list had its own sub-list:

It was irresponsible

We could be caught

There might even be security cameras

It would be harder to forget it happened when I was in that same room for meetings at least twice a week

If I were looking at any other dilemma with as many red flags, I'd say that proceeding shouldn't even be considered. But the one thing that kept me pinned to the table, the pro that outweighed all the resistance combined, was actually a question that contained only two words—*what if?*

*What if* this was my only opportunity to explore this side of myself?

*What if* I never met anyone willing to try to dominate a dominant?

*What if* Boyd wasn't a boy at all when it came to the bedroom?

*What if* he was exactly the person I was looking for?

And so I stayed put and waited for him. Even as the *tick-tick* of my watch indicated I'd now been waiting for sixteen minutes. With each second that passed, more doubt crept in, but so did the excitement for the possibilities. So did my arousal.

It didn't hurt that my undergarments were laid across Hudson's chair. Passive-aggressive, yes, but a big fat *screw you* to his company policies and personal rejection all the same.

After twenty minutes had passed, though, I had to face the reality that I'd been stood up. With a soft groan in my throat and a bowling ball of disappointment in my gut, I began to push myself to a stand.

"Face on the table." Boyd's voice came from behind me, more authoritative than ever.

It sent a delicious buzz down my spine and sent my body back into place. "I was beginning to think you'd had second thoughts," I said, my heart racing furiously.

"If this demonstration is going to be a success," he said, his words deep and measured, "there will be some rules you must follow. First, no more thinking. Second, no more talking."

He was still in the shadows behind me where I couldn't see him. I wondered how long he'd been standing there, watching, waiting for me to tire of waiting. It unnerved me enough to let his commands prickle. "Those are pretty big—"

He cut me off. "I'm standing in the doorway, Norma. Say another word and I'll turn around and leave."

My jaw clamped shut.

Several silent seconds passed before he said, "That's better. Now, if you absolutely need to say something—that you need me to stop, for example, or that you're in some sort of pain—then you will knock against the table three times in rapid succession. Knock once now if you understand."

I hesitated, pulled in separate directions by the urge to tell him off and the need to *get* off. The increasingly itchy spot between my thighs kept me silent. I knocked once.

"Good girl." His praise kindled an old familiar fire. The one that flamed and licked with each *A* I'd gotten in school. With each promotion at work. With each acknowledgment of success.

Yes, I was a sucker for approval. I rarely got that anymore. I was the oldest sibling, the head of my department, the lead in everything. My life lacked recognition, and the intensity of my craving for it had gone unrealized until now.

And like a moth seeking light, I wanted more.

My mouth wet with anticipation, I tucked my chin into my chest in an attempt to see the man who was affecting me so completely.

He'd dropped his jacket on the seat of Hudson's chair and was now almost finished rolling up the sleeves of his dress shirt. When he'd completed his task, he dropped his hand to my panties, lightly sweeping his fingers over the crotch. The gesture made my eyes widen and my pussy throb. I gasped softly, capturing his attention, and he turned to see me watching.

With his expression tight, he moved around the table until he was at my side. Then he reached out and lifted my chin from its cocooned position, bending so we were eye to eye.

"This is how you are to stay, your body still. If I catch you watching me again, there will be consequences. Understood?"

I'd never seen him so determined, so in control. My lungs constricted with the weight of his threat. *Consequences.* Consequences were for people in positions beneath me. Consequences were what my father had threatened me with in his drunken rages. Consequences were not fun or sexy or something that should ever sound enticing.

And yet it did.

When Boyd said the word, and with that glint in his eye, it was as if he were talking about candy, a delicious chocolate truffle that I shouldn't have, but maybe just one. If I were brave enough, I would have challenged him. Would have forced him to show me what he meant by *consequences.*

But I wasn't—yet.

So I knocked once.

"I knew you'd learn quickly." The pride in his tone did something strange to my insides, made me feel squirmy, yet I wanted to be perfect for this. I wanted to be perfect for *him*.

He moved out of my line of vision, and my desire to please warred with my curiosity. Damn, I wanted to know what he was doing. I strained my ears, listening, and every hair on my body stood up in anticipation. I heard the roll of a chair on the carpet, followed by the fall of his footsteps, and a moment later I sensed him behind me. The warmth of him radiating up the back of my legs to my center. My very naked—very wet—center.

After what felt like an eternity, his hand circled around my calf. With a firm tug, he nudged my leg until my shin bumped against the wood of the table. I bit my lip so as not to make a sound, but my inner sex kitten let out a surprised little squeal as Boyd wrapped a thin familiar material around my limb and secured me to the furniture, pulling my torso forward as he did. Surprised, I sat up without thinking and peered over my shoulder.

Or maybe I *was* thinking and I just couldn't help myself. Couldn't help sneaking a peek. Boyd was still bent at my foot, tightening the knot in the unknown fabric. A glance at the chair where I'd left my stockings solved the mystery—they were missing. *Clever boy.*

I wondered if he'd realized that this particular table had legs or if he'd just gotten lucky. He'd been specific about using conference room B—how observant was Boyd, anyway?

And why did I even care about that when the man was now pulling my other calf toward the opposite leg of the table?

I let out a squeak as Boyd delivered a sharp smack on the outside of my thigh. "Head down, Norma."

That sharp, no-argument tone combined with the sting of his slap made me even wetter. Soon I'd be dripping, which wouldn't be as big of a deal if I weren't now in such an exposed position. My dress still covered my ass, but spread like this—my legs wide and stretched, tied to the table legs, no panties on—I'd never felt more vulnerable. Or aroused.

Or this out of control. It was an unusual feeling, though not entirely uncomfortable. I just didn't know what to do with it. Didn't know how to give into it. Didn't know how to let myself relax.

Boyd seemed to sense my anxiety. He circled a hand around each of my ankles, his grip firm and hot.

"Take a deep breath in and out." He waited as I did. Then ordered me to do it again. "You remember your signal for if you need me to stop?"

My heart skipped with trepidation as I tried to imagine what he might do to me that would require me to have a safe word—er, safe *knock*. For whatever reason, maybe because I relied on him so thoroughly in the office, I trusted him. I rapped once in the affirmative.

"Good girl." Again, his praise shot a thrill through me. "Three times, and I'll immediately take my hands off of you. No questions asked."

He'd take his hands off of me? Well, fuck if I'd use that signal then. In fact, I was wondering what I'd have to do to get him to spank me again…

"Stop thinking, Norma." Seriously, how did he know? "Just concentrate on what I'm doing. Let go of everything else."

I tried to push all thought aside as his fingers began skating along the insides of my legs, so soft that it almost tickled, so slow that I could pour ketchup faster. Up, up, up, his hands danced along my skin, stirring my blood as they climbed past my knees, over the curve of my thighs and toward my center. When he reached the creases where my limbs turned into pelvis, I held my breath and waited for his touch to land in that spot—the spot where I wanted him most.

He didn't land there.

Instead, his hands flew off of me, returning to my ankles. I let the air out of my lungs in a disappointed sigh. But then he started a new trail up my legs. Slower this time. Lighter. So very deliberate and titillating. My skin had tingled on his first journey—now it was on fire. Every part of me felt hot and needy. By the time he reached the top, I was fighting not to squirm, biting my lip to keep from making any noise. It was torture.

The worst part, though, was when he skirted the lips of my pussy, his fingertips nearing my clit, closer, closer—

Then, for the second time, his hands were gone.

I whimpered and immediately tensed, afraid my outburst would invoke a *consequence*. But if his next torturous voyage up my skin was meant as punishment, he didn't say. It was agony either way. His hands moved so feather-light that sometimes I couldn't tell if he was actually touching me. My nerves buzzed, my muscles ached from the wide stance, and my pussy did, in fact, drip—a detail not missed by my tormentor when he finally, finally reached the inside of my thighs.

"I like that," he said, the rasp of his voice increasing the itch of my desire. As he slid up the slick skin of my slit, I began a silent prayer that he'd reach the prized spot this time.

Because if he didn't, I was absolutely positive that I would die.

What I didn't realize was that he'd wound me up so tightly that I nearly died when he *did* reach my clit. Just one brush of his fingers against the swollen nub, and I couldn't help myself—I moaned.

"Sorry," I said breathily, and then I almost said sorry again for saying sorry, but managed to catch myself, biting the inside of my cheek.

Boyd's hand stilled, but he didn't remove it—*thank god*. "You can make sounds," he informed me. "As much as you want. I like hearing you. Just no words."

I moaned again in relief and then in ecstasy as one of his fingers began moving again, sweeping circles over my clit with the slightest bit of pressure, just enough to send me toward orgasm, but not enough to let me release. I wanted him to push harder. I wanted him to slide his hand lower. I wanted him to finger-fuck me like he meant it. I didn't just want that, I needed it. I began to writhe and buck, urging him to move there.

Boyd stood and put his free hand on my lower back to keep me still. "Goddammit, Norma, I swear, if you move again, I'll make sure you're tied so tightly to this table you can't move and you'll have to take all the punishment I give."

Feisty with frustration, I lifted my head. "Will you spank me again?"

Instantly, he leaned in, gripping me firmly at the back of my neck, his mouth hot at my ear. "No. You'd like that too much. But if you defy me again, I'll start over. How would you like that?"

Now that would be true punishment. One I could not handle, especially not now that he'd spoken to me in such a dominating manner. I'd been on fire before, now I was burning.

I shut my mouth, knocking once to let him know I understood, wishing I had some way to let him know how desperate I was. I had a signal for yes and a signal for stop, but I didn't have a signal that said "put your fingers inside me and let me come for the love of God." He also didn't know that the only way I'd ever been able to orgasm was with clitoral *and* G-spot stimulation. There was no way I'd get there until he penetrated me in some way.

Boyd released my neck, returning to rub the small of my back. "Trust me. I know what you need." He didn't, but I'd agreed to let him do this. He'd find out soon that it wouldn't be enough, even if I didn't tell him. Even if I didn't direct his every move.

And if he didn't, well, then I could still say I gave it the old college try. I forced myself to let go.

As if to prove himself, Boyd increased the pressure with his finger on my clit and let his thumb skim across my entrance. My pussy throbbed and my insides clenched.

Oh, holy hell, I was close—closer than I'd thought possible without him inside me. So agonizingly, torturously close. I began to whimper, my chest so tight that I could barely get a breath as I climbed higher and higher. When I thought I couldn't take it anymore, he dipped his thumb inside my hole, just the tip, and ohmygod, to my delighted surprise, there I was, soaring over the edge into the oblivion of ecstasy. My legs shook, my ass shimmied, my entire being shuddered with the roar of my release, every single cell in my body screaming in pleasure.

I was still spinning through the clouds, vaguely aware of him tugging my bindings free, when he yanked me by my hair to a standing position, turned me into him, and bent to crush his mouth against mine. His kiss was insistent, demanding. Greedy. His lips were both soft and firm. He tasted like almonds and mint and power, and I'd never tasted anything so good in my entire life.

My orgasm began to fade, and I was already imagining what the rest of the night would be like. My sister, Gwen, was working. We could go back to my place. Or rent a hotel, if he preferred. Someplace with room service. We'd order champagne and strawberries and do all sorts of kinky things with the whipped cream.

He began to pull away, and I reached my hands around his neck to hold him still. But he gripped my wrists and pulled them down.

"You have a lot to learn about what I want to give you." His voice was controlled and unaffected, despite his erection, a steel rod, against my belly. "I'd like to teach you, if you're willing to be taught. You decide."

Brusquely, he let me go.

Then he turned and left.

# Chapter Three

The next day I woke up with my head in the clouds and an ache of desire that I'd never known. Before the fog cleared from my brain, when I was still half asleep and blanketed in images and sense memories from the night before, I let my hand slip lower, lower, to the V between my thighs. I found the lips of my pussy and began to part them, wanting the pressure on my clit.

Then suddenly I remembered.

Remembered that this fantastic afterglow had been courtesy of Boyd Barrett. Remembered that he'd changed from a quiet, subservient boy to a taunting, commanding man. Remembered that he was eight years my junior. Remembered he worked for me, and in two short days, I'd have to face him again in the capacity of his boss.

I could never go into work again.

Okay, that was an exaggeration. I loved my job too much to even consider leaving it in jest for more than a handful of seconds. The next option—transferring or firing Boyd—was also one I couldn't think about for long. I'd gone through a series of very bad assistants right before I'd hired him. Each time I'd had to find someone new, the next few months were miserable as I taught them the ropes and got the new hire accustomed to how I liked things. Which I was particular about. Because, yes, I was hard to work for, and I knew that.

And that was why I could not, would not, live without Boyd. In my office, anyway. And that meant I couldn't follow through with any other fraternization. Last night should have never happened, and it certainly could not ever happen again.

Fantasizing about him with my hand down my panties wasn't going to help nip that in the bud either.

I groaned and threw the covers off of me, heading for the shower. Usually I ran first, and I still planned to, but I needed something to cool the fire in my veins. Hopefully standing under an ice cold stream of water would do the trick.

It didn't.

I tried running next, opting for ten miles instead of my normal six, thinking maybe I could sweat out the lust like it was a cold. Or was that a fever? Whatever, I came back tired, achy and soaked in perspiration, and the buzz between my legs was stronger than ever.

I was distracted by it through the rest of the morning. Gwen and I caught up on *America's Got Talent* before she planned to go to bed for the day—her job at a nightclub kept her on a strange schedule. Afterward, I couldn't remember a single thing I'd watched, but I could recall with clarity every moment I'd spent with Boyd the night before. That wasn't a subject I planned on discussing with Gwen, though. So most of my responses to her were nods and grunts. Then she'd gone to sleep, thankfully, except after that I was left alone with the agony of my desire.

The rest of the night was more of the same, and Sunday as well. By Monday morning, I'd run over twenty miles, cleaned my entire house, taken five showers, and *not* thought about Boyd Barrett about a thousand times. Maybe even two thousand times. And now I had to go to work and face him.

Help me God.

I decided to go in early. That way I could sneak into my office without having to pass him on the way in. It wasn't until I was in the elevator on my way to my floor that I remembered I also didn't want to see Hudson. Several years with a clean, respectable work record, and in one evening I'd shattered my reputation with not one, but two, colleagues. The two colleagues who were the most important to me, no less.

Jesus, maybe I *did* need to quit.

It wasn't yet seven, but it wouldn't surprise me if Hudson were already working. Often, he slept in the loft above his office, which made an early appearance more probable than one from Boyd.

Anxiety rose in my chest, an odd feeling for me since I was usually composed and calm. As soon as the doors opened, I ducked my head and scurried down the hallway, letting out a sigh of relief when I made it past Hudson's office without seeing him.

And then gasping sharply when I ran into him, instead, outside my own office.

"Norma, I was hoping you'd be here early. I wondered if I could have a few minutes of your time."

*Oh, fuck.* This was it. He was going to bring up Friday night. He'd even come to my office to talk instead of calling me to his like usual, probably so he could remind me of my place. Or for some other psychological reason that I hadn't figured out yet in my head.

Strangely, I wasn't that anxious about it. I was more worried about Boyd.

Glancing past Hudson to make sure my assistant wasn't yet here, I said, "Yes, sure. Come on in. Let's talk."

"Excellent." He followed me into my office and made himself comfortable while I turned on the lights and booted my computer.

When I was ready, I pasted on a confident smile and said, "Shoot." I braced myself for the firing, sure that he wouldn't actually let me go, but worried I'd want to when he was done.

But, instead of scolding, he said, "I'm having second thoughts on the Pershing purchase. Can we reevaluate that before we complete the sale?"

And just like that we were back to normal. Which was why the confrontation with Boyd worried me more. I'd guessed there was a good chance that Hudson would pretend my advances never happened and would treat me just like he always did. He was good at compartmentalizing. The master.

Boyd, on the other hand…

I didn't know yet how he would be, but it wasn't him I was concerned about—it was *me*. How the hell was I supposed to face him without blushing? Without feeling squirmy and overheated? Without wanting more of…well, of whatever it was he wanted to give me. Which I absolutely should not want. Or act on. Or even dream about.

Fortunately, my meeting with Hudson was distracting. And it was brief enough that he was gone before anyone else arrived. As soon as he left, I shut my door. As if that would hide me from Boyd. I laughed at the idea.

Then I sat down, and when I could finally get myself to focus on something other than my assistant, I threw myself into work.

It was almost ten when my phone rang. I reached for it without thinking, so when I heard his voice on the other end, I was completely unprepared, even though every call that came into my office went through him first.

"I wasn't sure if you'd gotten in yet or not." Of course he wasn't sure. I usually only kept my door closed when I was out or when I was meeting with someone.

"I'm here," I said, my voice squeaky and as uneven as my pulse. "I didn't realize it was so late. I should have let you know. I came in early to get some extra work done. On the Sallis deal. And the, you know, the other, whatever…" I was a babbling idiot, and I couldn't stop myself.

He came to my rescue, attempting to mask any humor he felt from my chatter. "It's fine, Ms. Anders."

Had the way he said my name always sounded so naughty? As if I were a teacher, and he were my student? My attractive, extremely well-built, sexy student. Damn, that was hot.

No. It was not hot. That needed to be my new mantra. *Not hot. Not hot. Not hot.*

"That's great. Thanks, Boyd." I slapped a palm over my eyes as my face heated with humiliation.

"I have some contracts that the courier dropped off for your signature. Should I bring them in to you now?"

"Should you bring them in?" This shouldn't be a hard question. "Uh. Yeah. That might be okay." Except, I was already slick in the panties just from his voice. How the hell would I survive his actual presence?

"So yes, then?" He sounded so much more confident than I did, even to myself. Bastard.

*Get your shit together, Norma.*

"Yes? I mean, yes. Completely yes." Confidence. I could do that. That was a thing that I had sometimes. "And just come on in. The door is unlocked."

I hung up and sat on my hands to stop from calling him back

and telling him I'd changed my mind—about him coming in my office, not about him "teaching me." But that too. Definitely that too.

Then the handle was turning, and he was walking into my office looking like the same old Boyd Barrett who'd worked for me for a year now. He wore his glasses, and I suddenly decided that I had a thing for a man in spectacles. And floppy hair. Who was half my age. Okay, three-fourths of my age. Whatever. It felt significant. Significant enough to know it was inappropriate to let him affect me so entirely.

And now he'd said something, and I had no idea what it was. In fact, I was pretty sure I'd just been sitting there with a dopey look on my face the whole ten seconds he'd been in the room. But now he was looking at me, awaiting a response, his expression showing no hint of what had occurred on Friday night.

Well, shit. Maybe I was overreacting to the whole thing.

Regroup.

I took a deep breath, and as much of an idiot as it made me appear, I asked, "Sorry. My thoughts were elsewhere. What was that you said?" I'd left a lot of room for him to walk in on the comment about my thoughts being elsewhere, but I forced myself to hold my countenance, hold his gaze, and be cool.

"I just said that I'd marked the pages you need to sign with tabs. Page seven needs a correction before you sign, but I put that on the sticky too."

Man, he was perfect.

Strike that. He was a perfect *assistant*. And if he was perfect anywhere else, it would be someone else who discovered that. Not me.

Still, my hand was shaky as I scrawled my name on each marked page while he waited. I scanned the page he'd said needed to be amended, and sure enough, he was right. So perfect. And not hot.

When I finished, I handed him the stack. "Will you please make sure that Hudson's team gets that correction?" I waited until I'd finished my sentence before looking up at him, afraid if I didn't, I'd trip all over my words again.

Then when I lifted my head, my stare smashed right into his crotch, which—with me seated—was eye-level. Which was ridiculous to take note of because he'd stood right above me like this, how many times? And the crotch had never been an issue before in the least.

Blushing, I averted my gaze and stared at the now empty space on my desk where the papers had laid just a moment before.

"Of course. And I'll bring that section back for your signature before submitting them." Even with the slightest trace of amusement in his voice, Boyd was every ounce the professional that I should have been. That I usually *was*.

"Great. Thank you." I turned to my computer screen, essentially dismissing him. It felt rude somehow. But I was kind of sure that was how I usually treated him. Wasn't it?

Whether he was offended or not, he took the cue. At the door, he hesitated. "Would you like this shut again?"

I gathered my answer this time before I stuttered a response. "No. You can keep it open." I didn't sound certain, but I couldn't hide behind my door forever.

"Got it." He started out then paused, his head half turned away so that I could study him more freely than if he were looking right at me. His jaw was sharper than I'd realized before. Square. Strong and smooth, though Friday he'd had the slightest hint of stubble. I wondered what that might feel like along the inside of my thigh, how it might burn and tickle and drive me crazy.

Then he was talking again.

My head snapped to attention. I was pretty sure he'd said something about having one more thing. So I said, "Yes?" Which felt like it would work in a variety of situations in case that *wasn't* what he'd said after all.

He locked his eyes with mine, slamming the breath out of my lungs with the intensity of his stare. "I just wanted to say for the record, Ms. Anders, that this is your court. Here, you're in charge. Like you've always been."

It should have been awkward to have to be reminded of my place by my assistant of all people. But instead, it was comforting, which was surely how he'd meant it. His expression was intent. His tone sincere. He wanted us on familiar ground as much as I did.

And wasn't he the gentleman for giving us permission to do just that.

"Got it," I said, repeating his last words.

He winked—an action that absolutely did not send a storm of butterflies to flutter in my belly—and disappeared from the threshold.

Well. That was over. And everything was fine. We'd be fine. Work would go on just fine.

Also, now I'd learned a few surprising things:

After this exchange with Boyd, remaining professional with Hudson would be a breeze

Boyd wouldn't make our working relationship awkward by bringing up reminders of Friday night or trying to encourage a repeat

Any move that happened between us would have to be orchestrated by me

I was also ninety-nine point five percent certain that eventually a move *would* be orchestrated by me. The question was, how long could I hold out before that?

\* \* \* \*

The answer was *nearly six weeks.*

It was the end of August, and Boyd had accompanied me on a business trip to Montreal for a few days, as he often did. As I'd suspected, things had returned to normal in the office. Boyd had maintained his professionalism, never making sly remarks or even throwing a crude glance my way, though I threw more than a hundred in his direction. We never talked about that night or his proposition. We were good. Stable.

But I did find myself taking more notice of him in those weeks. His careful attentiveness to his job and my needs as an employer seemed to be layered with more than just the desire to perform well. There was care involved. There was interest. There was affection. All of which grew quietly between us and our glances became longer and more frequent and the magnetic pull between us grew stronger.

And so, sometime after dinner that evening in Montreal, I found myself outside his hotel room wearing nothing but the white robe that had been provided in my suite. My hand was surprisingly steady as I knocked, and when he opened the door, it was a relief to finally say, "I'm ready."

# Chapter Four

Boyd wasn't wearing his glasses, so when he looked at me standing in front of him, I could easily see his eyes spark and then darken. His mouth turned up into a small smile, and without a word, he stepped aside and opened the door wider to let me in.

A sudden burst of shyness overcame me. I tightened the belt around my robe and stepped inside tentatively. As soon as the door was shut behind me, he grabbed my wrists and wrapped my arms behind my back as he pushed me against the wall.

He leaned his forehead against mine. "What took you so long?"

The agony in his voice matched all that I'd felt in the past weeks, and relief swept through me to realize that I hadn't gone through it alone.

"Didn't know how to approach you in my court." I was dying to touch him, to pull my hands away and stroke his face, to run my fingers through his messy waves of hair, or, God, to caress the planes of his bare chest. His grip was too tight, though, so instead I tilted my head forward, desperate for my lips to brush against his.

But he pulled his head away before our mouths met. "We have to set up rules and boundaries." He dropped my arms and walked backward cautiously, peering at me as though I were something to be afraid of.

And maybe I was. I was certainly afraid of the way he made me feel, of the woman he turned me into—a woman with no thought or interest but getting naked with a man she shouldn't be glancing twice at.

After a second, Boyd seemed to gather his wits, chuckling to himself as he scratched the back of his neck. I took the opportunity to check him out. He was wearing dark blue pajama bottoms and nothing else, and seriously, I'd known he was built underneath those dress shirts he wore to the office, but I'd had no idea he was built like *this*. His chest was toned in all the right places, his abs sporting a six-pack that would probably be an eight-pack if he hadn't just eaten dinner. He had those to-die-for V lines that some men have—the ones that did weird things to my insides when I saw them in photos on Tumblr and absolutely sent me into a sea of lust when I saw them in person. A thin patch of dark hair dusted his lower abdomen, trailing down below the drawstring of his PJs. I wanted to trace that hair like it was the upward line on the latest Pierce Industries financial sheet, wanted to see the reward at the end. His arms were all muscle, his biceps surprisingly developed. I had no doubt he could lift and carry me somewhere, say, the bed, where I would straddle him and find exactly where that trail led. With my tongue.

"Norma?" Boyd nudged my attention back to him. Or, rather, back to what he was saying. He'd crossed to the small round table next to the window and still had his hands on the back of the chair he'd obviously pulled out for me to sit in. "Want to take a seat?"

I'd much rather bend across it like I had in the conference room, but apparently that wasn't yet on the agenda. I pursed my lips. I was all about following agendas. I just wasn't used to the agenda not being mine.

Boyd smiled knowingly, as though he could read my every thought. "Talking is essential before we go anywhere else. That night—the one at the office—it shouldn't have happened."

My eyes blazed, and I couldn't decide if I was angry, humiliated, disappointed, or a combination of all three.

He must have understood my expression because immediately he amended his statement. "I don't mean that it shouldn't have happened altogether—I'd never want you to think I meant that. I meant that it shouldn't have happened without a conversation first. If we'd talked, maybe it wouldn't have been so long between then and now."

Warmth rekindled in my chest, and hesitantly, I relaxed my guard.

"So come over here so we can get on to..." He paused, his eyes scanning me hungrily. "Other things."

That was the invitation I'd needed, and without consciously deciding to move, I found my legs carrying me over to the chair. I sat, relishing the light contact of his hands brushing across my back as he removed his grip. He moved out from behind me, heading not to the seat across from me but to the room's mini-fridge. He pulled out a bottle of white wine, uncorked it, and returned with it and two glasses.

"I don't usually encourage alcohol for this discussion, but I think a little might be helpful this time."

"How often have you done this? And, actually, what is this that we're doing?"

"I've done this—had a conversation about the type of relationship I was interested in having with a woman—three times. This will be the fourth." He'd poured a glass while he'd talked, and now he slid it toward me. "As for what this is—well, that's what you and I have to decide."

He poured a glass for himself, but I suspected he had no plans for drinking any of it. He'd never touched a drop at any of the business functions I'd attended with him over the year, even when he was most definitely not on the clock.

I, though, as he'd suggested, needed it. I quickly drank half of my glass before attempting a response. "Are you going to pull out a contract now and ask me about my hard limits?"

"I didn't take you for the type to read romance novels," he laughed, and I realized that he did that easily. At work, he was always serious and straight-laced. I'd never glimpsed this lighter side of him. I'd never glimpsed this take-charge side of him either. Obviously, there were a lot of layers to Boyd Barrett that I'd yet to encounter.

"I don't read romance novels. I read one novel. *The* novel." When he didn't drop the amused expression, I added, "Everyone was reading it. I wanted to know what the fuss was." The fuss, I'd decided—for me, anyway—had less to do with the type of sex that the characters had engaged in and more to do with the way the hero dominated his heroine in just the precise way, understanding what she needed and wanted better than she did half the time.

"And, wait a second. If you know about that, are *you* reading romance novels?" That should have been my first thought. Obviously, I was distracted by wine and half-naked Boyd and open discussions of sex.

"I saw the movie on a blind date."

Was it weird that I was jealous?

My face must have betrayed my emotions because he said, "She was an awful date—spent the three hours after the movie telling me all the differences from the book. I took her home and never went out with her again, but I do like the way jealousy looks on you."

He winked, and the way he smoldered when he did made me lose both my breath and any shame I might have had for being so transparent.

"Anyway," he said, growing serious. "I don't have a contract, but yes, we can discuss limits if you like. I'd actually prefer to approach that more as we go, much like a typical monogamous relationship between a man and a woman."

"O-kay," I said, drawing the word out. *A typical monogamous relationship.* It had been so long since I'd had any relationship with a man that I wasn't sure I knew what typical was anymore.

I really did have a lot to learn.

Silence settled between us, and I wondered if there was something I should have been doing or saying that was "typical." I took another sip of my wine, and when that didn't inspire me, I asked, "Are you waiting for me to say more?"

He smiled mischievously. "I'm waiting for the alcohol to take effect."

The alcohol was already taking effect. I was a lightweight when it came to drinking, and Boyd knew that. "That's a bit sly of you, isn't it? Should I be worrying that you're going to take advantage of me?"

"I believe that's exactly what you want." He said it low and confidently, the same way he'd spoken to me that night on the rooftop, and damn if it didn't get my hormones jumping. "But if you need reassurance, I am not going to take advantage of you. I'm not even going to touch you. Not tonight anyway."

And now my hormones were shrieking in horror. "Then I think you've misinterpreted why I'm here." Maybe this was why he thought

I needed the wine—so he could let me down easy.

"If I have, I'll be gravely disappointed."

Attempting to read him, I caught his gaze. It was hot and heavy; it was as filled with lust as I imagined mine was. It was reassuring enough to return my hormones to a pleasant buzzing.

Or maybe I was buzzing because Boyd had stretched his hand across the table and was now stroking up and down the inside of my forearm. Both the gaze and the touching were nice, I decided.

"Let me tell you what it is that I want," he said, his eyes tracing the pattern his fingers were making on my skin. "A monogamous relationship, as I said before, but much like you are my boss at the office, I'd like to be your boss in the bedroom. More than the bedroom, if you're up for that, but it's a good place to start."

I swallowed. "My boss? Like, you want to tell me what to do in the bedroom? Like I'm your sex slave?" Not that I was exactly opposed. I just needed clarification.

"Not a slave. Closer to a submissive, but not in all things. There are areas of your life I'd like to have authority over. Which areas are mine is what needs to be discussed. We need to draw boundaries."

That was better, actually. I'd be kidding myself if I thought I could ever be anyone's slave, even just in the bedroom. Submissive, though…that was maybe more in line with what I was looking for. An opportunity to stop thinking and just feel.

But if we were going to draw boundaries, I needed to have my wits about me, and that wasn't going to happen as long as he was touching me like he was.

I pulled my arm away, brushing my hair behind my ear as an excuse. "I'm guessing you have some ideas already in mind."

He nodded. "Obviously, the office is your court. I don't want anything to change with our relationship there."

"Good. That's a hard limit." I smiled too widely at my own joke—the wine was definitely relaxing me. "What do you want authority over? Just sex?"

"Sex, definitely."

God, I was already squirming, and he'd only *said* the word. I couldn't begin to imagine what it would be like when we were finally doing it.

"Also your evenings in general. We'd eat dinner together. Go on dates occasionally. Sometimes we'd stay in." His tone was such that there was no denying his innuendo.

I probably should have been alarmed about the idea of giving someone *authority* over such a big portion of my life, especially when I still wasn't quite sure what all the arrangement entailed.

But I was a smart woman. I knew that if I wanted my life to be different than it had been, I had to try something new. So I dived into my area of expertise—negotiating. "My sister is off on Tuesdays and Wednesdays. I spend those nights with her."

"No Tuesdays or Wednesdays. Got it."

"And Sunday nights I usually have a lot of prep for the work week."

"I'll take your Sunday days instead."

How easy it would be to start fantasizing about Saturday nights with Boyd, followed by lazy sex-filled mornings.

*Focus, Norma.* Boundaries. Negotiate. "I often have business functions in the evenings."

"I manage your schedule," he reminded me. "I know exactly what you have and what times you'll be available for me."

I wondered if he saw me shiver. "So I'd spend every other evening with you?"

"Not necessarily. But you'll be available to me then if I ask you to be. I might give you notice or I might not. I might call, and I'd expect you to answer. Whatever else you have planned, you'd drop it, even if it's just because I said so."

"Oh." It surprised me how arousing the scenario sounded. So fucking arousing.

"Sometimes I'll want you to stay the whole night."

Did I mention that he made it all sound arousing?

Again, I had to force myself to focus. "Can I be back before six in the morning? That's when Gwen gets home, and I'd prefer to not tell her about any of this. The less people know, the better. Because of work."

"Back before six. I can do that. You might be tired." His smile was devilish.

I swallowed. "Okay."

"I'd want to choose your underwear."

I was somewhat taken aback. "Do you not like my underwear?"

"I'm sure I like it just fine, Norma. I've seen very little of it to know. But I'd like you to be thinking of me every time you're touching the most intimate parts of your body."

This time my shiver was more of a delicious shudder. "Okay," I said again. He was so good at rendering me speechless.

"Now, if you don't follow these rules, Norma, there will be consequences."

"Consequences? Like, punishments?" I'd grown up with an abusive father, so the idea of punishments made me slightly wary.

"I'm not a sadist. So my punishments aren't any more painful than a hard spanking. Maybe a belt now and then. Or a wooden spoon. Or, if you'd prefer, punishments can be withholding pleasure."

"I don't mind spanking. Or a spoon. No belt though, please." That had been my father's favorite method of discipline.

"No belt." Boyd's expression said he understood, and I was sure he probably did. He knew about my father, having fielded calls regarding his present incarceration for child abuse. "You'll tell me if there are other things that you don't feel comfortable with, okay?"

"I promise."

"Good." He studied me for a moment then said, "I like bondage. And blindfolds. And toys."

My face felt warm. Hell, my whole body felt warm. "Me too." Then my cheeks felt even warmer because I had no idea what I was talking about. "I mean, I think I do too. I've never…well, I've tried toys, but…"

His blue eyes turned dark and inky. "What toys?"

"A vibrator on occasion. That's all."

"I'd like to watch that sometime."

My breathing felt shallow and rapid, and if we kept discussing this much longer, I was sure I would jump out of my skin. Especially when he looked at me like that, all silky and seductive and simmering.

I blinked, needing a break from his intense gaze and the even more intense conversation. "Is it weird that we're just talking about this so openly?"

He shrugged, his eyes continuing to bore into me. "I don't think so. I think it's hot."

"Yeah. Hot." *So, so hot.* I was pretty sure all he had to do was say *orgasm* and I'd do it. I was that turned on.

I reached for my glass and downed the last swallow of my wine. "Is there anything else?"

"Like I said, we can work it out as we go, just like any other sexual relationship. Right now the only real thing we need to agree on is whether or not you'll let me own that part of you."

*Own.* When he said it like that, so pointedly and plainly, it made me hesitate. Not because I didn't want to say yes, but because I *so badly* wanted to say yes that I was afraid of sounding too eager.

And, also, I was a little bit scared.

But I'd been scared when I'd helped prosecute my father for beating up my little brother, Ben. I'd been scared when I'd entered a field dominated by men. I'd been scared when I'd accepted my entry-level position at Pierce Industries. *Scared*, in my experience, just meant it would be worth it.

Finally, I dared to answer. "Okay." It sounded less sure than I'd have preferred, but there it was, and I meant it.

His face lit up, and my entire body lit up with it. He stretched both his hands to clasp one of mine between them, and his expression grew solemn. "This won't be easy for you, Norma. I know that. The work situation only makes it trickier. I know your job is your priority, and it's mine as well. *You* are a priority to me. I don't just care about sex. Every aspect of your life is important to me. The relationship we have right now is important to me. I don't want to lose any of that. I want to add to it. I want more."

Well, those were words I'd replay a million times in my head. I was the oldest of three kids, and with my mother's death and my father's asshole version of parenting, I'd become the person who supported my siblings. I'd sheltered them and fed them and clothed them and consoled them. At work I'd quickly climbed the ladder to chief financial advisor where I managed and directed others. I'd never been the one being managed or cared for. I'd never been anyone's priority.

If I were the type of person who cried, I might have gotten teary then.

But I wasn't, even with the wine in my blood. I was moved, though. Then I realized what deep words like Boyd's meant. "That sounds like a boyfriend."

He tilted his head. "Is that a problem?"

Romance as well as sex? It was both appealing and terrifying. I was good at quick decisions when I had to be, but this one needed time. If we added emotions to our relationship, how much harder would it be to break it off when it inevitably grew sour?

On the other hand, what if that risk was worth it too? "Maybe that's one of those things we can work out as we go."

"I can accept that. Just know that I'm going to romance the pants off of you." He grinned, and had I been wearing panties, I was pretty sure they would have melted.

With a laugh, I said, "You obviously don't need romance to get my pants off."

"You just don't realize how much romancing I did to get you here."

It was my turn to tilt my head and study him. "You're a totally different person from the one I know at the office. It's like, you wear your glasses and you're one guy. Take them off and you turn into this."

"I assure you they're both the same person. The guy who puts the contracts on your desk and screens your phone calls thinks about you naked as intensely as I'm thinking about it right now."

His brazen declaration was such a turn-on. It made me feel unusually coy, which I hoped read as flirty rather than bashful. "You think about me naked?"

Again, that grin. "Don't *you* think about me naked?"

*All the time.* But all I could manage was a nod.

Silence fell, and this time it wasn't an awkward space waiting to be filled with words. Instead, it begged for action. In each aching second that passed, the tension stretched between us and the electric charge in the air grew hotter. I twisted my hand in Boyd's so I could lace my fingers through his and wondered if other parts of our bodies would fit so perfectly together. So snugly.

Just when I thought I couldn't take the yearning a moment longer, Boyd withdrew his hand from mine. "It's time you go back to your room."

Oh, yeah. He'd said something about not touching me tonight. I'd hoped that was simply a statement to put me at ease. My voice felt husky as I said, "I could stay."

He stood and came to me, extending his hand to help me up. "No, you can't."

"Why not?"

He was so close now, standing right in front of me, his eyes pinned to my mouth. I swept my tongue across my lips, wetting them.

His expression grew stoic, controlled. "Because I said so and that needs to be enough when we're in my court."

I cocked my hip. "It's my first day. I'm new. Throw me a bone and tell me why anyway."

"Because I need to take my time with you, Norma, and that will take mental preparation on my part."

Besides excelling at negotiation, I was very skilled at persuasion. I took a confident step toward him. "You were perfect that night at the office without mental prep."

"I prepped long and hard for that night, believe me. It just took a while for an opportunity to arise to put my preparation to use."

"I bet you're just as good at the spur of the moment."

He ignored me, raising his voice slightly to take command. "More importantly, you initiated being here tonight. Which I'm very happy about. It needs to be on my terms for this to be what I want and what you need."

"Then give me your terms. I can abandon my own." It didn't escape me that I was chasing him, and that this was exactly the sort of pursuit I was tired of. I was just so full of want and need that I couldn't seem to stop myself.

"My terms are that you stop trying to tempt me and go back to your room tonight." His tone was sweet and charmed, but also tight, and I wondered if that meant his self-control was wearing thin.

Time to move in for the kill. I untied my robe and let it fall from my shoulders, baring my naked form. "I don't *want* to stop trying to tempt you."

The flicker of desire across his face was the only warning I had before Boyd grabbed my wrists and pulled me abruptly to him. He kissed me, roughly, passionately, dominantly. He kissed me until I was out of breath and so wet I had to press my thighs together to stop from dripping.

Then, just as abruptly, he broke away. "You are going to try my restraint, aren't you, Norma?" His voice was raw, threadbare. "The only reason I'm not punishing you for this is because I don't think I can be around you for another minute without throwing you on the bed and claiming every inch of your gorgeous body."

"That was exactly what I was going for. Do it. I'm ready."

"No. You're not." He dropped my wrists and tugged my robe back over my shoulders. As he retied my belt, he whispered, "Not for what I want to give you."

I'd always loved a challenge. Always loved proving people wrong—proving *men* wrong. "I *am* ready." I moved closer and palmed the bulge at his crotch.

Oh. My. He was even larger than I'd guessed when I'd felt him pressing against me.

Boyd chuckled as he pushed me away. Again. "And that right there proves that you really aren't ready." Gripping my shoulders, he spun me so my back was to him.

I groaned as he walked me toward the door. "I don't understand. I want you."

He sighed behind me then brought his mouth close to my ear, so close his breath was hot against my skin. "I want you too. You have no idea how much." He rubbed his nose against my lobe before nipping at the sensitive skin. "But when I fuck you, Norma, I have to know that you're going to let me lead. And I don't know that yet."

Goose bumps sprouted on my arms and a delicious thrill ran down my spine at his talk of wanting and fucking and leading. Then he stretched past me to open the door and gently nudged me out.

"I'll watch you until you get to your room," he said, kissing me on the forehead.

Begrudgingly, I shuffled the three doors down to my suite, and when I chanced one final glance in his direction, the protective, possessive look on his face warmed me so deeply, it burned away any trace of disgrace I might have had at my dismissal.

Oh, yeah, this was definitely going to be worth it.

# Chapter Five

The next day, Boyd and I met for breakfast in the hotel restaurant before our meetings for the day. We didn't have much time to talk before some peers from the conference joined us, but he did manage to tell me that he'd communicate by text in the future so we wouldn't have to risk mentioning our relationship out loud, especially at work.

"Keep the times we agreed upon free," he said, "and I'll let you know in the next few days when and where I want you."

*When and where he wanted me.* I wanted him anywhere. I wanted him now.

But I had a feeling he meant to teach me patience. Especially when he made me wait almost a full week before texting me an address and a time.

It was a Thursday, and he'd given me no time for running home to change after work, so I arrived at the Chelsea apartment wearing the same thing he'd seen me in all day. I'd put on sexy panties that morning, just in case, but I worried about that too since he'd said he wanted to dictate what underwear I wore then never mentioned it again.

That concern occupied my mind as I took the elevator to the eleventh floor and walked the short hallway to his unit. Then when he opened the door, I couldn't help blurting out, "You never told me what to do about my underwear."

He laughed, standing aside to let me in. "You won't be wearing any for long."

His statement made my legs so weak, I wasn't sure how they carried me inside. Combined with the yummy way he looked in faded jeans and a T-shirt, his feet bare, I was surprised I was even able to breathe normally. Fortunately, he took my hand, which helped keep me upright, and tugged me toward the kitchen island.

"We'll pick out some bras and panties later online," he said as he half leaned, half sat on a barstool and began undoing the button at the cuff of my sleeve.

"Okay." But now I wasn't really paying attention to what he said because I was checking out his apartment.

It was nice. *Really* nice.

The floors were hardwood, the kitchen modern and stainless steel. I didn't know how many bedrooms there were, but the living space seemed large.

"Uh, Boyd," I asked, barely noticing that he'd moved on to my other wrist. "Excuse me for maybe speaking out of turn, but there's no way you can afford this place on the salary I pay you. Are you a male escort or something in your off time?"

With a slight grin, he pulled me closer and began unbuttoning my shirt.

"I definitely couldn't afford this on my salary. But I have other money."

I started to ask the source of his "other money" but was stopped by his finger to my lips.

"We can talk about it later. Right now, I don't want you to say anything at all. That's your punishment for trying to seduce me in Montreal. I haven't been able to stop thinking about your naked body all week. You can't imagine how many hard-ons I've had to hide at the office."

I was more intrigued than ever about his income, but now he'd distracted me. "You've had hard-ons at the office?"

"Norma, no talking." He wrapped his hands in the material of my now open blouse and pulled me closer to place a kiss on the space between my breasts, just above my bra. "I need to thoroughly explore my possession, and to do that appropriately, I require total concentration."

I opened my mouth to either protest or purr—okay, it would

have been purr; the idea of being owned by him made me all sorts of turned on—but Boyd shushed me with a stern look before removing my shirt the rest of the way. Silently, he unzipped my pencil skirt and pushed it down over my hips and to the floor. He swept his gaze over me, and without the permission to talk, I realized for the first time in my life how often I hid insecurity behind conversation. It was so much easier to stand nearly naked in front of a man when I was allowed to comment.

I reached out to him—if I couldn't talk, I had to show him how much I wanted to touch him. But he grabbed my wrists, stopping me. "No talking, no touching. In fact, as soon as I have you all the way undressed, I'm going to chain your hands to that hook behind me. Do you see it? Nod if you do."

I peered past him into the living room and found a large hook fastened into one of the beams that crossed the ceiling and a link chain hanging down from it. An anxious thrill bubbled in my chest as I nodded in the affirmative.

"Good," he said, and heat spread through my body at his praise. "All I'm going to do is tie you and touch you. If you can't keep yourself from talking, I'll gag you as well, but I'd prefer to have your mouth free." He noted my expression and added, "Not for what you're thinking, naughty girl. I want you to be able to speak if anything I do bothers you. If you need me to stop."

"You want me to use a safe word?"

He frowned at me sternly. "Do I need to gag you?"

"I'm just trying—" *to clarify*, but I stopped myself when the look on his face told me that he would let me know everything I needed to know if I'd just be quiet. "No. You don't need…" Dammit, I was still talking. "Sorry," I whispered. Then mouthed another apology when I realized that whispering still counted as talking.

Underneath his disappointed glare, I sensed he was amused by my inability to shut up. "If you need me to stop, you'll say 'stop,'" he said when he was certain I was done making a fool of myself. "Other times we may need a safe word. But for now, that will be enough. Nod if you understand."

I nodded, biting my lip to prevent any unwanted speech from slipping out of my mouth.

"Good girl."

God, if he just spent the rest of the night expressing his approval with me, I was pretty certain that it would be the best sex I'd had in a long time. I loved hearing it, loved hearing him praise me in that tone of voice that said he was genuinely pleased. Loved it so much that it made me confident enough to stand proudly as he stripped off my bra and panties.

He didn't say anything more when I was naked in front of him, but the crotch of his jeans bulged, letting me know he liked what he saw. Without words, he led me to the living room to stand beneath the hook in the ceiling. On the couch lay two silk scarves and a set of leather handcuffs with a metal link chain between them.

"Hands, please," he said, and I held them out for him. He wrapped a cuff around one wrist and tightened it until it was snug then repeated it on the other wrist. Then he fastened the clasp on the end of the chain hanging from the ceiling to a link in the middle of the chain on my cuffs so my hands were stretched and suspended above my head.

He looked me over, seemingly pleased with my appearance. Then he pulled off his T-shirt and tossed it aside before grabbing one of the scarves off the couch.

I was tempted to remark that, in his faded jeans and nothing else, he looked quite like the hero from that one book—the book everyone had read—but the scarf was of more interest. "What's that for?"

He glowered. "This one's to blindfold you, but the other is in case I need to keep you quiet." He moved to stand right in front of me, so close that his chest brushed across my nipples. "I've been so looking forward to touching every part of you, Norma," he whispered, "and I know you could love it too. But I promise it will be so much better if you're silent. Just be a good girl and let yourself feel, okay?"

I let out a long breath before I nodded. It shouldn't be so hard to keep my mouth shut, and maybe he'd hit the nail on the head— maybe all the talking kept me from having to feel. In my lifetime there had been so many feelings that I'd wanted to avoid. Perhaps I handled them all now—turned them, inspected them, made them safe and sterile before putting them on.

I didn't want to live like that. Not if it meant missing out on the feelings that Boyd wanted to introduce to me.

So I let out another breath as he tied the scarf around my eyes and resolved to be a model submissive for the rest of the night.

Boyd spent the next fifteen minutes, longer possibly, doing just as he'd promised—touching me. He ran his fingers along every inch of my skin, then his lips, then his tongue, leaving no part of me unfelt or unexplored. With my sight gone and without the crutch of conversation, the rest of my senses perked up. My arms ached from being above my head for so long, but it became background sensation as I tried to guess where he'd go next, listening and feeling the heat of his body near mine, my muscles tensing in expectation. Over and over, he surprised me, and each startling caress notched my arousal up another level, even though his hands barely grazed my most erogenous zones.

I'd had almost no experience with Boyd yet, but I was sure of one thing—the man was an excellent tease.

As he fondled me, he'd praise me, commend me, admire me. "You're so tight," he said, spreading his hands over my ass, and I mentally applauded myself for all the miles I'd run over the years. Then his mouth was on me there, licking down to where my cheek met my thigh. "I could live with my face right here."

God. What would that be like? I'd be happy to find out. Even happier if he'd move his tongue to the space *between* my legs. I widened my stance, hoping he'd get the hint, but he only chuckled and continued with his own damn agenda.

Just as the thrum at my core and the pain of my outstretched arms became too agonizing to remain silent, Boyd pulled me against him and angled his mouth over mine. He drank my unuttered cries, shaping my lips to mold with his. He slid his tongue across mine. Over mine. Around mine. He tasted familiar, like victory and mastery and promise, the way a newly acquired dividend looked like it would taste. In that kiss, I forgot about other lips and flavors and even about the other wants and desires licking their bold flames inside of me.

Then he pulled away. The silk scarf came off of my eyes, and there he stood in front of me, his eyes burning with lust, his cock a firm rod tenting his jeans. "I should get dinner ready for us," he said.

And, yes, I was hungry. But food was the furthest thing from my mind.

"That's all?" I hadn't meant to sound so annoyed. No, actually, I had meant it. "Not that I don't appreciate the attention, just—"

He'd reached up, presumably to unhook the chain of my cuffs from the ceiling, but he paused before doing so. "Did I say you could talk yet?"

I flushed but pretended that I hadn't. "You said we were done, so I assumed. Though, I'm not sure how this can be done when no one actually finished." *Ouch*. The words stung as I heard them with my own ears, but it was too late to take them back now.

Boyd didn't seem to feel the sting. Instead he looked at me with growing curiosity. "*No one actually finished...* You mean because no one came?"

"Yes, that's exactly what I mean." Talking about it pushed my need for release even higher.

"We can fix that." Boyd dropped his arms and began undoing his jeans.

My mouth watered, and it didn't matter what the rules were regarding speech, because I couldn't have stopped myself from babbling if I'd wanted to. "God, Boyd, I want you. Please, let me have you. Please." I'd never wanted to see a cock so much in my life. Never wanted to touch it so badly that I salivated.

"I am letting you have me." He pulled down his briefs just far enough to let his erection spring free. I gasped at how hard he was, how big he was. Boyd Barrett was hung. Who knew?

*I* knew. *Now* I knew, anyway, and damn, I'd never been so excited about an endowment as I was about this one.

My eyes were pinned to his hand as he circled his palm around his throbbing staff. "This is for you. All of this." He pumped his hand down his length. "Watch me stroke myself. This is only because you asked for it. Because you wanted me so badly."

I pulled at the chain above me, desperate to have his cock. "I want you inside me, Boyd. Let me have you. Let me suck you."

"No."

My heart tripped over that one word. I must have heard him wrong, surely. "What?"

"This is what I want to give you, Norma. This alone." He continued to stroke himself as he spoke, and I suddenly understood he had no intention of giving me what I so eagerly wanted.

"No! Please! Boyd!" I was unable to make a complete sentence, my words falling out in short, staccato pleas of frustration.

"Appreciate this, Norma. Watch this. Keep watching. I love your eyes on me while I jerk off. Almost as much as I love looking at you while I do it. It's you that's made me so fucking hard, and I'm going to come even harder. All for you."

God, oh, god. I was clamping my thighs together, trying to stifle the strength of the pulsing while at the same time begging for Boyd to ease it in other ways. "Please. Please. I want you. Please!"

His strokes came quicker, his hand moving faster and faster along the length of his erection, the muscles in his forearm growing more taut and strained.

"Tell me where you want me to come," he said, his voice tight as it interrupted my hoarse appeals.

"What?" I was having a hard time concentrating.

"On you or in my hand. Tell me where to come." He took a step closer to me. "Hurry, Norma—decide."

*Where to come.* He wanted me to decide where he should come. His expression tightened, and I realized what he was asking as his face contorted with the onslaught of his orgasm.

"On me! On me!" I pushed the words out just in the nick of time, arching toward him to catch every drop of the hot stream of his climax on my belly. He groaned as he came, his lids heavy with ecstasy, his body tense as he emptied himself.

Hell, it was the most erotic thing I'd ever seen. I almost came just from the sight.

When he was finished, we were both sweaty and breathless. And the way he was looking at me now, his expression sated and oh so pleased at the artwork he'd left on my skin—I could live forever with that gaze, even if I never got off myself.

Okay, maybe that wasn't quite true. I was more aroused than I'd ever remembered being, but somehow, his release felt more gratifying than I knew an orgasm of my own would have felt.

He reached above me to unhook my hands and said quietly, "You'll stay the night tonight. I didn't prepare you to stay, but there's no way I can let you go home. I should have everything you'll need."

I was shaking as he brought my arms in front of me to undo the cuffs. There was so much I wanted to say, so much I wanted to ask him to do to me, so much I wanted to beg for him to let me do to him.

All I could manage was, "Okay."

He nodded once, the subtext behind his eyes seeming to understand all that I'd left unspoken.

Then, he tucked himself away, and said, "Let's clean you up."

# Chapter Six

Boyd took me to his bedroom suite and left me to shower with instructions not to get myself off, which was especially maddening because I hadn't had the idea until he'd brought it up. Then it felt like the most erotic agony as I washed my body, purposefully ignoring the buzzing between my legs. I'd been dealing with that unfulfilled yearning for weeks now and had assumed that I'd have some relief after agreeing to a relationship with him. But at the moment I was more miserable than ever.

Yet, I was in a surprisingly good mood. My shoulders felt less tense than usual, even after having my arms suspended for so long, and my body hummed with a tune familiar and long forgotten. There was even a bounce in my step as I toweled off and stepped out of the bathroom.

The bedroom was empty when I came out. I put on the T-shirt that had been laid on the bed, assuming it was meant for me, and followed the delicious smell of garlic and rosemary to the kitchen. I'd figured Boyd had ordered Italian, and so I was surprised to find him standing behind the stove, an apron over his bare chest and jeans.

I sat on a barstool and smiled at him across the island. "You cook?"

He poured me a glass of red wine and then dumped some into the saucepan in front of him before glancing up at me. "Sometimes. Right now I'm cooking for you."

"I can't remember the last time anyone cooked for me. Maybe my mother? After she died, I was the one who made all the meals." I still made most of the meals for Gwen and me. Or, rather, I ordered most of the takeout.

"You work too hard all day; you shouldn't have to cook at night too. I'm glad I get to be the one who changes that."

I slanted my gaze at him. His floppy hair hid his brows, and even though he didn't look up, I could see the grin on his lips. *Perfectly shaped lips.* Not too full, not too thin. Exactly right for kissing.

I bit my own lip thinking about the feel of his mouth against mine. "You really are good at that romance thing."

"Don't get too excited. It's only spaghetti."

Yes, except the sauce was homemade. And, from what I could tell, it looked like he was making up the recipe as he went along. And he had me daydreaming about making out when I'd never been big on kissing before.

Something caught in my chest, and I had to change topics to something less sappy. "So now that I've had your cum all over me, I feel like we're close enough for me to ask how you can afford this amazing place."

He glanced up with a chuckle. "You asked me that before you had my cum all over you," he said, bringing the sauce spoon up to my lips to taste. "By the way, you looked really hot like that."

"Mm." The sauce was good. What he'd said was better.

It was my turn to grin. "Now you've flustered me. I can't remember what I was saying."

"Lies. You don't forget anything." He moved the pan of boiling pasta to the sink so he could pour the noodles into a colander. "You were asking about my money."

He paused and I wasn't sure if it was because he was focused on his cooking or because he didn't want to say more. I was curious, though, so I waited quietly, which was easier than usual to do.

When he'd finished straining the spaghetti, he grabbed a plate from the counter that he must have laid out earlier, since it already had a serving of salad and a breadstick. "It's a boring story, actually," he said, using tongs to drop a pile of noodles on the dish. "I inherited everything. My father founded his own tech company, a very successful tech company. He passed away a few years ago and now it's all mine." He scooped a spoonful of sauce on top.

"You own a tech company?" I asked, taking the plate from him when he passed it over.

He dished up his own serving next. "I own shares in it. My brother and sister and I all own a third."

"Then why the hell are you working for me?"

"Are you complaining?"

"Noooo." I stretched out the end of the word so he could know exactly how much I wasn't complaining.

He took off his apron and threw it on the counter before grabbing two forks out of a drawer. "Are you judging then?" His tone was playful but pointed. "Is it better to slave away all day and night for a business that I don't have a passion for just because I have the opportunity to be important in that way?" He picked up his plate and his own glass of wine then gestured for me to come with him.

"No judging." I slid off the barstool, teasing him as I followed him to the living room. "Defensive much?"

"Sorry. I hear this a lot. I have years of preparation with my response."

"Then give it to me. The fully prepared response. Not because I'm judging you but because I want to know everything about you."

"Now who's doing the romancing?" He set his dishes on the coffee table then turned to take mine from me. "You don't need to respond to that. Just let it sit and niggle at you until it's comfortable."

"Go on..." I smirked, aware of the niggle. Not exactly sure how to feel about the niggle.

Instead of sitting on the couch, as I'd assumed he would, he sat on the floor and leaned back against the sofa. "My father worked his ass off for that company. And for all the money and influence it got him, it also brought him enough stress and turmoil to ruin three marriages and put him in a grave before he was fifty-five."

I swallowed, the story sounding too much like one that could be my own.

But it wasn't my story. This was Boyd's story, and I wanted to hear more.

Curling my legs up underneath me, I sat down next to him. "I'm sorry to hear he's gone."

Boyd shrugged, spinning spaghetti around his fork. "I don't miss him. I know that sounds terrible, but I didn't even know him." He opened his mouth to take his bite.

I took the opportunity to do the same. We ate quietly for several minutes.

After a while, when we'd finished half our meal, and as if he hadn't been silent for more than a second, he said, "That's the part I'm sorry about, really. That he was never around. He hungered for that success, and he got it, at the loss of everything else." With his thumb and index finger, he wiped sauce off his lips. "I decided a long time ago I never wanted to be that guy. I'm fortunate to have money. It gives me the opportunity to do whatever I want."

I took a sip of wine and raised a brow. "And you want to be the assistant of a pretentious bitch?"

"Well, I didn't know what you were going to be like when I took the job."

I narrowed my eyes, and he reached out to run the back of his knuckles across my cheek. "I'm joking, Norma. I like working for you. A lot."

I took a shaky breath in, my body growing warm.

Thankfully, he dropped his hand before I overheated. "I like business," he said. "I know a lot about it. I didn't have a head for the tech stuff, but I was great with the numbers, and I spent a lot of summers working in the financial department of my father's company. That's where I discovered how satisfying it was to put in a full day of meaningful work and then go home and not have to think another second about payroll and unsigned contracts and projects that I should have followed up on. Without that burden, I have time to pursue the thing I'm really interested in."

"Which is…?"

"You."

Never mind not overheating. I was in full *too heated* mode now, feeling more like I was wearing a sweatshirt than a T-shirt. "Be serious."

"I am being serious." He was looking at me—I could *feel* his stare—but I couldn't look at anything but my plate.

He bent down to catch my eye. "You're going to have to get

used to me saying that I've wanted you, Norma. Because I have. And I do. I'm not going to hide that when we're together like this. Okay?"

I nodded, not sure if I could speak.

"Good. And okay, it wasn't always you, specifically. Before I met you, I'd been interested in pursuing a serious relationship that involves an exchange of power. With that as my goal, and in order to maximize the potential of that sort of situation, I decided I couldn't have a career that would distract from that. I chose to find a job that didn't drain all my time and energy so that I could put all of that into this."

I studied him a moment. I'd never given much thought to Boyd and his career except to hope that I never lost him as an assistant. It was thrilling to have this view of him. He was magnificent and assertive in so many ways I'd never noticed before. Strong-willed, even. More like me than I had imagined. "You were born with one kind of power and craved another."

He considered this, amused. "I guess that's one way to look at it."

I pondered my own quest for success. "I didn't have any power growing up. I had nothing. I think I thought that if I was perfect, if I worked harder, excelled at everything I did, that it would make up for all the shit years of being powerless. That I could make a difference for Gwen and Benjamin. That I could make up for the happiness we never had."

"Did it?"

I'd been mulling half to myself and was almost surprised to hear him chime in. It took another second to digest his question. "It's nice to have things now that I didn't, I guess. But sometimes I think there's something missing." A lot of times, actually.

"Maybe we can fix that together."

There he was with the romance thing again. This time I managed to hold his gaze. "Maybe." But what I meant was, *I'd like that.*

Then, because I'd *really* like that, I pushed my dinner plate away and scooted closer to him. I was as hungry for him as I'd been earlier—more now, possibly—and I was one to go after what I wanted. Somehow I'd forgotten.

The scent of him made me dizzy as I nuzzled at his ear. "You know, I can stay tomorrow night too," I whispered. "If you'd let me know now, I could be ready. Pack a bag or whatever."

With a cocky grin, he turned into me, his lips hovering above mine. "It's your job to be ready anyway." *Oh, yeah. That.* "And you really don't need a bag. You can always steal my clothes." He tugged at my shirt. "Or you could just be naked. That would be fine too."

Yes. Naked would be more than fine. "No bag, then. The point is I can stay tomorrow night." I tilted my face up, intending to capture his mouth with mine.

But Boyd only let my lips brush against his before pulling away. "I'm sure you *can* stay since that's one of my evenings. But that's not for you to decide." He set his plate down on the table behind him. "I'll ask you over *if* I want to and *when* I want to. Got it?"

He didn't even raise his voice, but immediately my eyes pricked. I'd been chided and rejected, and now I remembered why I hadn't gone after what I wanted until now—because that wasn't how this was supposed to work between us.

"I did it again, didn't I?" With a sigh, I lay back on the floor and willed the burning in my eyes to go away. "I'm sorry, I'm not good at this." Translation: I'm stupid and small and inadequate and a terrible submissive.

A tear slid down my cheek.

*Crying? What the hell?* I never cried. Not when I thought about my dead mom. Not when my father beat my brother, Ben, to a pulp. Not even when Ben tried to kill himself. Crying was not something powerhouse businesswomen did. It wasn't something *I* did.

Quickly I wiped the tear away, then the next one, hoping they'd gone unnoticed by Boyd.

No such luck.

"Hey." He stretched out over me, drawing my hands above my head, forcing me to look nowhere but at him.

God, his body touched mine everywhere and it was *incredible*. He was firm and tight and, um, hung—I was pretty sure that bulge at my hip wasn't even all the way erect.

And while I was daydreaming about his girth, he searched my face. "You think that's not partly why I'm interested?"

My lips bent into a pout. (At least I was done crying). "You like me because I'm bad at the kind of sex you're good at?"

He laughed, an easy sound that was freer than anything I'd heard in a long time. Had I been that happy-go-lucky at his age? I didn't think so. Had I ever been?

"Oh, Norma," he said soberly, brushing the hair from my face. "Stop thinking and listen to me."

I peered up at him, suddenly feeling younger just because of the way he looked at me, all serious and knowing. Affectionate, too.

"I like the challenge, yes." He placed a kiss on my chin. "And I like that you're smart." Another kiss, at the shirt's collar. "And confident."

He gripped the hem of my shirt—*his* shirt—then pulled it over my head. He paused to admire me, causing my cheeks to get hot.

"And you're so strong." He bent to draw my nipple into his mouth, sucking it to a taut peak before letting go. "And driven," he said as he moved to repeat the action on my other breast.

"And you have all this power." He slid down my body, laying a kiss on my navel, which ironically left me feeling weak and very power*less*. "There's almost no one over you, not just in the office, but the industry."

His next kiss landed right above the seam where my clit hid, sending a deep shiver through my body.

I was a goner, but before I was all the way gone, I managed to ask, "And it turns you on to top someone at the top?"

Boyd ran his tongue along my slit then answered without looking up. "It turns me on that I can give you the one and only thing you can't give yourself."

"What's that?" My voice was shaky, threadbare.

"A break."

Then talking was over, and so was pretty much thinking, as he buried his face between my thighs, licking and sucking and nibbling until I was coming. Coming hard and long, like I'd never come before, every muscle in my body trembling with pleasure.

Even when I was whimpering and spent, he still didn't let up, tracing designs along my thighs with his fingers before inserting one, then two inside me. He rubbed and stroked and caressed, inside and out, while his lips kissed along my pubic bone. While his hands teased me to orgasm. While he helped me let go, and he gave me a break.

# Chapter Seven

That was as sexual as we got that night. The rest of the time he did his romance thing where he was very sweet and intimate. I slept in his T-shirt, he in a pair of boxers, my body curled into his, his arms wrapped tightly around me.

We didn't get any further the next time he had me over, either. Or the next. He'd go down on me, he'd use his hands, he'd massage my body, we'd make out. It was wonderful and amazing, like I was a teenager holding on to my virginity and he was the man who respected it.

But it was also frustrating.

Because I wasn't a teenager. And I wasn't holding on to my virginity—not purposefully.

A month went by. Then it was nearly two, and even though I saw him outside of work a couple of times each week, Boyd still refused to let me pleasure him in any way, saying he wouldn't let me until I was able to "let go"—his words, not mine.

As far as I was concerned, I'd let go of a lot. I'd certainly had plenty of orgasms, and didn't that require letting go?

Apparently there was more I needed to release. More I needed to be taught.

I'd like to say that I was a fast learner, because I usually am, but unfortunately that wasn't the case with Boyd. Being in charge was just such a longtime habit, such a hard one to break, that I casually gave orders and resisted domination without even realizing it.

Over and over I'd try to decide things for us. "I'll come over tonight," I'd say. Or, "I'll pick up Chinese for dinner." Always, I'd catch myself too late—or not at all—and he'd have to correct me. Which always stung, no matter how gentle his reprimand.

Sometimes my mistakes were even worse. Twice, I didn't put on the underwear he'd requested, simply because I hadn't been thinking, work already occupying my mind as I'd dressed. Both times he sent me home as soon as he discovered my error with instructions not to get myself off.

Both times I got myself off anyway. It wasn't like he knew.

Once, I made other plans on one of his nights without consulting him, not because I'd forgotten or because I'd been flippant about our arrangement, but because I'd honestly assumed he'd understand once I explained the situation. And maybe he did understand because he didn't make a scene when I explained.

He also didn't ask to see me again for an entire week.

Finally, one October evening before he left for the day—while we were still on *my* turf—I cornered him at his desk and asked him point-blank if he was still miffed about my alteration of the schedule.

"Miffed?" he asked, as if the idea had never even occurred to him. "Not at all. It just seemed that our arrangement might not be working out for you, and I was leaving you the opportunity to let it end without any huge upset in our working relationship."

"Because I swapped out one evening without asking first?" I was taken aback. Yes, I'd made mistakes, but surely that didn't mean I was a lost cause. I perched on the edge of his desk, signaling my willingness to talk about it further.

Boyd, however, stood and buttoned his jacket. "Not because of that one evening. Because time and time again, you step on my authority. As though it's not really an authority you recognize."

"That's not true at all." But as I said it, I knew it was a lie. "Well. I mean. It's not what I intended."

"Perhaps not. And I'm willing to overlook mistakes. But I'm not so amenable to your blatant disregard of the position we've agreed that I have over you. When you make light of that, it turns this whole thing we're doing into something petty and meaningless. That might be acceptable to someone else. Someone else might just be interested in a little roleplaying, a game rather than a lifestyle. A game is not what I'm looking for."

I thought about what he said while I watched him push in his chair and lock up his desk, thought about how I would have reacted if I had an employee that had not just made mistakes but had disrespected my command.

I thought about it and didn't like the conclusions I came to. Because I wouldn't have tolerated that for a minute. I'd have given walking papers right away. Boyd had been quite patient with me in comparison.

"I'm sorry," I said, looking down at my hands. "I hate being in the wrong, and I see that I am. I'm not unhappy with our arrangement. I'm somewhat frustrated with the pace of it—"

He interrupted. "It's meant to be frustrating."

I sneaked a glance in his direction and realized from his expression that I wasn't the only one keen to move things along.

At least that was comforting. "I know. I get that it's my eagerness that causes you to slow down even more. Point being, even with that frustration, I'm happy with what we're doing."

"You could be happier. If you let—"

"If I let go. Right." Why was that so hard for me? I couldn't think of a lesson that had taken me quite so long to learn. It made me even more anxious to learn it.

He towered over me when he stood up straight, and I had to peer up to look at him. Even this was difficult—being beneath him, asking for forgiveness.

But I wanted it—wanted *him*—badly enough to make the effort.

"Will you give me another chance?" I asked, my voice raw.

His lips parted slightly as he considered me, and I considered that mouth, wishing he'd kiss me, despite our location. It was well after five; no one was around. The cleaning crew wouldn't be in for another couple of hours.

"There's something in your tone that suggests you might beg if necessary." His eyes lowered to watch my tongue dart along my bottom lip. "It makes me awfully tempted to say no just so I can hear it."

My pulse picked up. Adrenaline coursed through my veins, and my brain started swimming with ideas that weren't wise. "Careful," I said, as much to myself as to him. "We're still in my court."

God, what I could do to him on my turf. Turn my position over him into one with a carnal element. Show him exactly how bossy I can get. It hadn't ever been a fantasy of mine, but he'd made me wait so long, I was getting desperate. Hungry. Yearning. All I had to do was stand up, press my lips to his...

As if he could read my mind, Boyd chuckled and took a step back. "I don't know about that. I'm officially off the clock. Hard to say whose court it is right now."

Oh, man. If the office turned into his territory—how many naughty things could he do to me? Turn the tables on my playground. Knock me off guard. I wasn't sure if I liked the idea or not.

He didn't make me have to decide, slipping out the door with only a wink, but I didn't miss the flash of struggle in his eyes, the single signal that maybe there were parts of this negotiation that he was unsure of too.

\* \* \* \*

Two nights later, he was more certain.

"You staying late?"

I frowned, looking up to find Boyd standing in my doorway, his jacket on, the room dark behind him. Didn't I *just* get back from lunch? A glimpse at the time on my computer screen said it was almost six. Huh.

I swallowed back a sigh. "Yeah, I guess I am. I really want to finish these reports up for the Donovan Tech proposal." There was probably another two hours of work on them. Maybe three.

I'd already shifted my focus back to the spreadsheet in front of me when he spoke again. "Don't you have until next week to turn them in?"

"But if they're off my plate, I'll have time to add my analysis to the real estate purchase Hudson is looking at."

"Isn't Mark the one assigned to that?"

I glanced up with a guilty expression. It wasn't as if Hudson had specifically asked me to give my opinion on buying the land, but I knew he'd appreciate it.

And I liked being appreciated. Call me brown-nose Norma.

"Ah, I see," Boyd said in a way that suggested he *did* see, that he was well aware my over-achieving nature was behind this and not any lingering romantic interest in my boss. Still, even though he understood, I couldn't quite tell if he supported my actions.

But this was my job, and I was the boss. His support was moot. "Workaholic," I said, reminding him who I was in case he needed it. "I can't be helped."

"I guess I'll see you later then." He smiled and gave a small wave, and my stomach tightened in the way it did so many times when I thought about Boyd.

This time when I turned back to my work, I was humming.

Barely five minutes had passed—at least, it felt like only five minutes—when my phone buzzed with a text. *Be in the copy room in ten minutes.*

The message was from Boyd. He only texted me when he was summoning me. When I was in *his* court.

*But it's Wednesday.*

I threw a glance to my desk calendar. Nope. It was Thursday. A *Boyd* day.

"Goddammit." Yes, I said it out loud. Even though it was entirely possible that he was outside my door somewhere within earshot. I said it out loud anyway because I was *that* frustrated. I'd *just* told him I wanted to stay late, and apparently he didn't care. Which was bullshit. I was not someone to be bossed around.

I was seconds from replying with exactly that when I reconsidered. His words from earlier that week replayed in my head. Words like *"blatant disregard of the position we've agreed that I have over you"* and *"seemed that our arrangement might not be working out."*

That was the whole point of us, wasn't it? For Boyd to boss me around. It was what I'd said I wanted. So did I or didn't I?

I hadn't quite answered that when another text came in. *Have your panties off and your skirt up around your waist.*

A shiver ran through my body.

Okay, I'd meet him. But I couldn't fool around on the premises. The night in the conference room had been risky enough. I'd have to put my foot down about it.

Another text: *Stop thinking, Norma.*

Right. Stop thinking.

Without responding, I saved the file I was working on and shut down my computer. Then I turned the lights off in my office, locked the door, and headed down the hall to the office supply and copy room.

It took three tries before I remembered the door code. I rarely ever needed it—I always sent Boyd to do the sort of tasks that required the use of this room. The delay getting in did nothing for my nerves. It was after hours and the entire floor was dark and quiet, but my heart was pounding so hard, I thought the inside of my chest would bruise.

I was there in time, panties on the counter, skirt hiked to my waist, but Boyd made me wait longer, that bastard. Try as I might to stop thinking, my mind raced those extra minutes with a million different thoughts. *Maybe he just wants to see if I'd do it. He might not even actually join me. Maybe he saw someone in the hall and is waiting for him or her to leave. If we got caught together, he could lose his job. The light in here is sure bright. No one should be naked under fluorescents. Wait. Is there a security camera in this room?*

I scanned the ceiling before remembering the only camera pointed at this room was outside, positioned on the door.

Boyd would have already thought of that.

*Relax, Norma. Trust him. Let him worry about everything.*

Even as I coached myself, I turned off the main light switch so the only source of lighting in the room was from the strip under the cabinets. It was better for the mood. Not that I knew what mood Boyd was going for.

And that was because it wasn't my business to know or decide.

With a sigh, I flipped the lights back on. He had to be so tired of me fighting him as much as I did.

Maybe he'd punish me for it.

I smiled thinking about that, and as soon as I heard the *beep, beep* of the code being entered, I pulled my skirt up higher and bent over the counter in case he needed the hint.

As soon as he walked in the room, he turned off the light. I had to bite back my grin. I *knew* it was better for the mood without it on.

"Norma," he asked after a beat, "do you think you're going to get spanked?"

"I'd deserve it if I did." I could feel him behind me, assessing me, his eyes on my ass, but I kept my gaze forward, pinned to the sleek Formica countertop.

He rubbed his hand over the curve of my behind. "But you're here. On time. Ready."

"I almost wasn't. I mixed up my days." I tensed, waiting for the smack—*wishing* for it. He'd only spanked me the one time that first night, and he'd said he wasn't big on punishment, but wasn't this a good occasion to make an exception?

*Mmm.* I hoped so.

But when his hand left my rear, it didn't return for the slap I'd braced for.

"Get up on the counter, Norma. You look gorgeous like this, but I'm not going to punish you for correcting your mistake. Anyway, it's not truly punishment if you're asking for it."

Pouting, I turned to face him. "I wasn't asking for it," I said, hopping up on the counter. "I was merely letting you know I was ready for it if that's what you wanted from me."

"Uh huh." His subtext was clear—he should be able to expect I was ready for anything he wanted at any time. That was our arrangement. "Let's talk about the bigger issue, shall we?" He slid his palms up my thighs, sending goose bumps scattering along my skin.

"There's a bigger issue?" I sounded intoxicated. Which made sense since I felt drunk just from this small touch.

And of course there was a bigger issue—I was still fighting his every attempt at control.

But I played dumb. "I didn't realize there were any issues. I mean, besides that I keep talking when I don't know if I have permission to speak."

"You can talk right now. We're having a discussion. And yes, there's a bigger issue." He smirked in a manner that made me feel like prey.

I swallowed. "Which is?"

"Which is…" His voice trailed off, his interest catching on the postal scale on the counter and the shipping supplies stacked on the shelves next to it. He grabbed a self-inking stamp, a red Sharpie, and clear packaging tape, then turned back to me.

He set the items beside me then pushed my knees apart so that my pussy was bared to him. "Why is it," he asked, reaching for the stamp, "do you think, that you mixed up your days in the first place?"

I shrugged, not sure where he was going with the question. "I don't know. Got absorbed in work, I guess. Sometimes it's hard to remember there's a world outside of that." I realized why he'd asked as I spoke my answer. "Oh."

"But there's a lot of world outside your office." He pressed the stamp against my inner thigh, leaving a red rectangular mark on my skin. He moved it up higher and stamped me again. And again. Then several times on the inside of my other thigh.

I didn't move to look at what the stamp said. It was too dark to see easily, and, anyway, I was transfixed by him—his mouth as he spoke, his hands as they moved with his task.

"There's a lot of world I'd like to show you outside that room, Norma." He set the stamp down so he could unbutton my blouse. Then he placed several more marks along my belly and along the top of my breasts.

Still, I kept my eyes on him.

He set the stamp down and reached for the roll of tape. "Give me your hands, please."

I held them out, not surprised when he bound my wrists together with several layers of tape, the sticky part facing away from my skin. Next he moved to my legs, wrapping my ankle to the handle on a cupboard below me, then my other ankle to another handle so my legs were spread wide.

When he was finished, I pulled against them, testing their strength, and found all of them secure.

"Too tight?"

I shook my head.

"Good." He nodded at me, his expression clouded with want. "All day long you sit at that desk, this is how I see you."

"Half-naked?"

"Or all naked. Depends on how willing I am to try to hide my erection." He sobered. "But I also see you tied. Tied to that office. Tied to that computer. Everything you do, every minute you exist in this building from the time you get here until the time you leave, you're tuned into the job. Sometimes even after you leave, too."

He meant *most times* even after I left. He was just too polite to say it, and I was too ashamed to correct him.

Boyd set the roll of tape on the counter then stepped back to study me. "Look at yourself, Norma."

Hesitantly, I glanced down at the words he'd stamped across my body. *PROPERTY OF PIERCE INDUSTRIES.*

My stomach dropped.

"You look pretty damn good like that, I have to admit. I'd be all over you every day if you didn't belong to *him*."

I hadn't been prepared for the jealousy that colored his tone. "Boyd…" I didn't know what else to say. I didn't know what words to give to assure him that the work that distracted me had nothing to do with Hudson and all to do with me. Didn't know how to explain that my actions said nothing about where my heart belonged.

And we weren't talking about my heart. We were talking about my attention.

There was nothing I could say to that because he was right—my attention *did* belong to Pierce Industries, ninety percent of my waking day. And once upon a time, I thought my heart did too. Now I realized that my emotions had only followed where my focus was, not realizing that there was someone much more capable of holding my affection than Hudson Pierce.

My head lowered, pulled down with the sorry I didn't know how to say.

"It's okay," Boyd said dismissively. "I can live with it. I can share you with him—like that—" He gestured to my tied hands, my marked skin.

"Because I know," he moved closer, picking up the red marker, "when you aren't his," he took off the cap and scribbled something over each of the stamps on my body as he talked, "when you take yourself off the clock, and you show up at the mere summons of a text message…" He leaned back so I could see that he'd changed each stamp to say *PROPERTY OF BOYD.* "I know that then you belong to me."

My voice felt trapped by the lump suddenly in my throat, but I managed to rasp, "I do."

"You work so hard…" He set the marker down then slipped his hands underneath my hair to knead the muscles of my neck. "I still like you tied up. I prefer it, though, when you aren't so tense."

"I'm already ten times more relaxed than when I left my office."
Seriously, I felt like putty in his hands.

"Let's go for one hundred times. Okay?"

I nodded, my body buzzing with anticipation. Whatever he had
planned, I knew I wanted it, knew it would be amazing.

He threaded his hand in my hair and tugged it back sharply so
that my mouth opened in a gasp that he swallowed with a languid
kiss.

Then he stepped back, so far back that he hit the workspace
opposite where I sat. He leaned against it, his hands gripping the
edges of the counter behind him. "Make yourself come, Norma. I
want to watch."

I hesitated for only a handful of seconds, seconds that were
filled with all the reasons not to do what he'd commanded, foremost
that I'd never masturbated in front of someone before.

But then I stopped thinking.

Because the look on his face said that was what *he* was thinking I
should do. But also because I didn't want to hesitate anymore. I
wanted to belong to him, just like he'd said I did. Like I'd said I did.

With my hands still bound, I pressed the tip of my finger against
my clit and rubbed it around in circles. I was awkward and
uncoordinated, but I was determined, and soon, the muscles in my
legs were clenching and my breathing had grown fast and shallow.

"Yeah. Good girl. Just like that." Boyd's attention was rapt, his
gaze on me as arousing as his touch ever had been. Especially when
he moved his hand to rub up and down the hard bulge in his pants.
"Are you wet?" His breath was as jagged as mine.

"So wet."

"Let me see. Stick your finger in your pussy and show me." His
eyes were fixed to me as I did as he'd instructed, and even though the
room was dim, I could feel his eyes darken when I pulled my finger
back out, covered in my slick wetness. "That makes me so fucking
hard, Norma. Did you know that?"

"*Mmhm*," I moaned. It made *me* hard, and I didn't even have a
dick.

"You're so beautiful, so ready, and I've been so patient." God,
the ache in his voice matched how I felt inside, mirrored my desire.
"I could fuck you right now. Would you want that?"

*Yes!* So much yes.

It was only one syllable, and I could barely get it out. "Yes."

"Here, in the place where you work? Is that where you want me to fuck you for the first time?"

"Yes." Anywhere. I didn't care that it was here. Just. Now.

Boyd unzipped his pants, and without undoing his belt buckle, he shoved his briefs down just far enough to release his cock. "I could take you right now. Slide inside you. Make this the place where you think of me." Instead of *him*—Boyd's meaning was clear.

It suddenly felt like all the weeks of longing had been building up to this moment, like there was nothing else standing between us. We'd discussed birth control (I was on the pill.) We'd discussed safe words (mine was "red" or three knocks.) We'd discussed the rules (unless I used my safe word, the rules were he could do what he liked with me.) The only thing that had remained in our way was me, and here with his eyes on me, his name on my skin, on my tongue—here I was so unaware of myself, it seemed impossible for me to still be any sort of barrier.

I arched my back, spread my legs as wide as the restraints allowed, a silent invitation. A desperate plea.

"But maybe I'm happy watching you." He circled his hand around his erection and tugged up. "I could stroke myself while I watch you come. I could come so hard from watching you make yourself feel good."

*No! Please, no.*

Disappointment buzzed above me like a fly looking for a place to settle, even as I rubbed myself harder, even as I neared climax.

"Would you want that just as much, Norma? Tell me."

I scraped my teeth along my bottom lip, looking for the *right* answer. "I won't lie—I want you inside me so badly I might die. But"—and this was also the truth, more the truth than I could express adequately with words—"I want what you're trying to build between us more. So whatever you think I'm ready for, that's what I want. That's what you should give me."

It didn't kill me as much to say it as I thought it would. It was actually beautiful to hear myself speak it, the way it's beautiful to let go of the string of a balloon, to give up the responsibility of holding it, watching it fly away and disappear into the sky.

With that thought, I hit my release—my *literal* release. I closed my eyes and let it throb through me, my movements stuttering, incoherent sound spilling from my mouth like it was being yanked out from inside me.

"Fuck, Norma." Boyd closed the distance between us in two strides, sliding his cock easily into my wet pussy, despite the resistance of my orgasm.

My eyes flew open, my breath hitching. He was there, inside me, so big and full as he pulsed against the walls of my channel. He was there feeling incredible, so much more incredible than I'd ever imagined. So worth every second he'd made me wait.

Maybe there was something to trusting his methods, after all.

He was still for several seconds, his gaze locked with mine as he let me adjust to him. Which was impossible because there was no adjusting to *this*—this monumental, indescribably full feeling that pushed at the inside of my chest even as my pussy stretched to make him fit.

"Boyd," I whispered when I could speak, because I had to say *something*, and there were no words at all worth saying but his name.

He responded by gripping the flesh of my ass, pulling me closer, shoving deeper inside me.

Automatically, my arms, still bound, flew up to circle his neck, and for the briefest moment, I worried that I should have asked for permission, feared I may have ruined everything.

But if he minded, he didn't show it. Instead, he began to move, pumping his hips against mine, driving inside me over and over. "I knew you'd feel this good. When I fingered you, I could tell you'd feel like this around my cock. Could tell you'd be this tight."

"I like it when you say things like that." Almost as much as I liked the sound of his balls slapping against my thighs and the spot he struck against with each thrust.

"I can tell by the way you grip me." Sweat beaded along his brow. "You like it because it's dirty or because it's praise?"

"Both."

"Yeah. That's what I thought." He silenced me after that, his lips capturing mine in a hot, searing kiss that was all consuming and brought me again to orgasm.

"I'm going to come with you," he grunted quickly, as though he were warning me, right before he exploded inside me with one long final push of his hips.

He pressed his forehead to mine as he caught his breath—or as he let me catch mine, which took a while. I was spinning, my thoughts and emotions in a whirlpool inside me.

Boyd ran his fingers across my cheek. "Are you okay?"

"Barely." I realized that wasn't very helpful when he leaned back to study me with wide eyes. "It's good. I promise."

His features relaxed. "Good." Then he was kissing me again, as tender as it was deep, as sweet as it was sexy. There were lots of things he was saying with that kiss, but my head was too jumbled to make much of it out—which, I had a feeling, was his intention.

Eventually, his kissing slowed, and he let words fill the spaces in between each brush of his lips. "So sexy," he said before nibbling on my bottom lip. "This was perfect. You're perfect."

"I like the way you kiss," I said when I had an opening. "That's not all I like that you do with your mouth, but I especially like the way you kiss."

"I'll have to kiss you more often."

"Only if you want to."

"I do want to." He pressed his mouth against mine as he spoke, as if to prove his want. "You deserve it. I'm especially proud of you right now. You did really good today, Norma Anders."

"Go on…"

He pulled back with a laugh. "You're such a greedy girl."

"You have no idea." I watched as he tucked himself away, my hands still wrapped around his neck. Then he slipped out from my embrace, kissing each of my wrists before reaching for my panties that lay on the counter.

"I wasn't planning this," he said as he used the silk material to clean me up. "Scratch that—I've planned this particular adventure for months; every time I had to come into the copy room for something, I imagined what I'd do to you in here. But I wasn't planning for anything to happen today."

He pocketed my now messy panties and grabbed a pair of scissors out of one of the drawers.

"Should I ask why you changed your mind?" I asked as he cut the tape at my wrists.

He shook his head. "It doesn't matter. I just wanted you to know that I *can* change my mind."

I had a feeling he meant it as another form of praise, but I didn't push him for more, letting him finish cutting me loose in silence.

When I was free, he buttoned my shirt and helped me down. "I can see the red marker through your blouse. Hope that's not going to bother you that people might see it while we're at dinner."

"We're going out to dinner?" Usually we stayed in, either at his house or mine.

"Yes. We are."

"I don't mind." It was exciting, actually, to be marked as his, to go out like that in public where someone close enough—the waiter, perhaps—might see.

He took my hand, threading his fingers through mine. "You know," he said, pulling me toward the door, "today is my birthday."

"No. What? Are you kidding me?" He started to twist the doorknob, but I pushed it shut again, wanting to talk about this without the security cameras. "Why didn't you tell me? I would have gotten something!"

"That's exactly why I didn't tell you. I never want to be another one of your obligations."

I smacked him, somewhat playfully, very intentionally. "I wouldn't give you a gift out of obligation. I'd give it because you mean something to me." Whoa. Had I really said that?

I had. And I liked how it felt to say it so I said more. "I'd give you a gift because I want you to know."

He reached out to trace the pad of his thumb across my bottom lip. "Trust me, I do know," he said softly. "You gave me the only gift I wanted."

I giggled, trying to reduce the intensity of the conversation. "What was that? A fuck in the copy room?"

"Your submission."

I swallowed. So much for lightening the mood.

I let him open the door then, let him lead me out of the room and out of the building. All the time, wondering if he realized that my submission had only been a part of my gift. Wondering if he knew that I'd also given him my heart.

# Chapter Eight

*Three Months Later*
*January*

Boyd's arm snaked around my waist as he kissed along my neck. "Are you sleeping?"

"Yes," I lied. I'd dozed a little earlier after Italian food and three orgasms, but I'd been awake for a while, drifting in happy thoughts while Boyd devoured the latest Robert Galbraith novel. He was an avid reader, I'd learned the last few months, another hobby that he insisted he was only able to enjoy because of his low-stress job.

"I knew you were faking." He nibbled at my lobe now, his hand cupping my breast.

I twisted to look at him. "How could you know that? I was as quiet as a mouse."

"Because, for the last fifteen minutes or so, you haven't been snoring."

I turned fully toward him so I could punch him playfully, but he predicted my movement and grabbed my hand at my wrist before I could make contact. I struggled even though I knew I was no match for him, and within seconds he'd wrestled me beneath him, pinning my hands to the bed.

"Damn, woman. I thought I'd worn you out earlier, but maybe you need another round to knock you out."

Um, okay.

And then the phone on my bedside table began to ring.

In unison, we glanced toward the sound. "Who the hell is calling you at one in the morning?"

"Ugh. Is it really that late?" I was going to be tired at the office the next day. Though strangely, for as much as Boyd kept me up these days, I hadn't had so much energy or been so productive since college.

"I'm sure it's Gwen." Boyd moved off of me so I could pick up the phone. My sister was pretty good about not calling while I was likely sleeping, but sometimes she lost track of "normal people time," understandable for someone like her who worked nights.

But a glance at the number said it was a California number. *Oh, God. Ben.* Instantly, the blood went cold in my veins—understandable for someone like *me* who'd once received a late night call from the San Francisco Police Department saying her brother had tried to kill himself.

"What is it?" Boyd asked, reading the panic in my expression.

I didn't respond, clicking on the "Talk" button instead. "Hello?" I sounded calm—I was sure of it—despite the dread tightening my chest.

A male voice asked, "Is this Norma Anders?"

I knew that voice. Scratch that—I knew that *kind* of voice. Authoritative, somber. The kind of voice that delivered news like, "Your mother didn't make it." The kind that said, "Your brother has to stay in the hospital to recover from the wounds inflicted from your father."

"This is she. What is it? Just tell me—is my brother okay?"

"Yes, ma'am. He's okay. But there has been an incident."

I chewed on my lip as I listened to the man—Dr. Evans, a psychiatrist at a hospital in San Francisco—tell me how Ben had again attempted to take his own life. He followed with basics about his condition, that he'd had his stomach pumped, that he should be fine but was being kept for observation to determine if he had liver damage.

"If he's okay, why is it you that's calling me instead of him?" It felt like my voice was shaky as I spoke, but when I heard myself, my words were even and collected.

"He asked me to call you." The doctor paused for half a second. "Because he doesn't want to talk to you himself. He'd also prefer not to see you or your sister, uh, Gwen. I've explained to him that since his mental health is in question at the moment, you may have the right to act on his behalf. He understands and assumes you'll fly out anyway."

I swallowed the sting of this latest news. *He doesn't want to see me.* "Where is he staying?"

"He's in room—"

I cut him off. "Hold on, let me get something to write this down on."

At once, Boyd held a pen and paper in front of me. He really was the best assistant.

I wrote down the room and hospital information from Dr. Evans as well as his cell number, then asked him for another recap of Ben's situation before I let him go.

"Your brother?" Boyd asked when I set the receiver back on the cradle.

I glanced over to find him sitting next to me on the bed, his expression calm but intent, his eyes trained on me.

"Yeah. He's in the hospital. Took a bottle of Vicodin, but then he changed his mind and called 911."

"You need to go there. Let me make arrangements."

Though Ben had told Dr. Evans he didn't want to see me, I needed to be there. There wasn't a thing I could think of that would keep me away.

Boyd was already grabbing for his laptop from the side of the bed. "I'll book a flight and a hotel. Do you want me to book for Gwen as well?"

"Oh, God. Gwen." My little sister was older than Ben, stronger, too. But still not as strong as she'd like to think she was. I worried about telling her almost as much as I worried about Ben.

With a shake of my head, I decided she needed to wait. "I'll call her later. Let me get myself organized first. And, no. I don't think she should come with me." I climbed out of bed and crossed to my dresser in search of underwear.

"You want to go alone?" Boyd asked from behind me.

My head was spinning, too many thoughts floating around, and though a clear plan of action was forming—get dressed, schedule a flight, pack a bag, call Hudson—I was barely holding onto it. Boyd's question nearly made me lose my strategy altogether.

"Not necessarily." I furrowed my brow, concentrating. *Did I want to be alone?* What I wanted wasn't relevant, was it? "I guess it doesn't matter one way or another. I just don't think Gwen should go. She's not the most positive influence these days. I don't think it would be good for her or for Ben right now."

I stepped into a pair of panties then worked on fastening a bra.

"Understood." His fingers click-clicked over his keyboard. "I'll just book for you. Then I'll arrange a car and help you pack your suitcase. In the morning, I can make sure all your appointments are rescheduled for the week."

I turned to face him, my jaw slightly slack. Boyd had just taken over more than half of my mental to-do list. It was a little unnerving.

But, also, it was a whole lot of a relief.

I took a deep breath and let a bit of the tension out of my shoulders. "I don't know what I'd do without you sometimes."

He'd donned his glasses when he'd reached for his laptop—turned out they were for computer work—and now he peered at me over the rims. "I could come with you. So you're not alone."

Time seemed to stand still as I considered. I didn't even know what to do with his offer. I'd been in these situations before, the kind that were hard and required tough words and a straight backbone. Every time, I'd been the one everyone leaned on. I'd been the one who'd kept things together. It was what I did. I did it alone.

I didn't know how to do it any other way.

"No," I said, finally and with finality. "That's not a good idea. I'll be distracted. You need to stay here and take care of things at the office." They felt like excuses for me more than for him.

He ticked his head to the side and stared at me. "I don't have to be in the office to take care of things there," he said gently.

My face wrinkled in confusion. I knew what he was saying, just, I didn't know what he *meant*. Would he come with me as Boyd my employee? Or Boyd my lover? What would it mean to us if I let him come? And what would it mean about me?

Before I could come to a conclusion, he'd set down his computer and crossed to me. He put a hand on each arm and bent to meet my eyes. "It was just an offer. Not a big thing. It's completely up to you. If you need me most as your assistant right now, then that's what I'll be. No explanation needed. Got it?"

I nodded as though I understood and I suppose I did, but I didn't too. I didn't understand why the offer was so unsettling. I didn't understand why I couldn't just take him up on it. Because while I didn't have much bandwidth to focus on myself, I was pretty sure I wanted him with me.

"I'll be right back." He kissed me on the forehead, startling me into action again.

"Okay. I, uh, need to call Hudson." Pushing Boyd and his offer out of my head, I crossed to the phone and pressed the speed dial for Hudson.

Even though it was the middle of the night, he answered on the second ring. "Norma. Is everything all right?"

"Yes." An automatic answer. "I mean, no. Sorry to call so late. It's…" I took a deep breath, gathering myself before saying his name. "It's Ben. My brother. He's made another suicide attempt—"

"I'm so sorry to hear that." His tone was reserved as always, but I could sense an undertone of compassion. If he didn't exactly care about me, he did appreciate me.

"Thank you. It's what it is. I just wanted you to know that I'll be out for the rest of the week."

"Of course. When do you want to fly out? You should take the Pierce Industries jet."

"Oh." For the second time in the last few minutes, a man had offered me assistance in a way that I hadn't expected. Again, I was taken aback. "Are you sure that's not too much trouble?"

"Not at all. I'll arrange it as soon as we're off the phone. I'll need a couple of hours. Should we shoot for an eight a.m. takeoff?"

"Perfect. Thanks." Through the chaos in my head, an interesting thought came through—why was it so much easier to accept help from Hudson than Boyd? Because Hudson was my boss? But wasn't Boyd my boss too?

I looked up at movement by the bedroom doorway and found Boyd returning, a mug of coffee in his hand. He crossed to me, handing the cup out in my direction.

So Hudson could let me use his plane. But what Boyd could give me was so much more what I needed.

I took the cup. "Uh, Hudson, also, I'm going to bring Boyd with me. Then I can get some of that Peterson project done while I'm there."

"Don't worry about—"

"No, I want to work." I met Boyd's eyes. "The distraction will be good for me."

"Are you sure?" Boyd asked when I'd hung up. "I want to be with you, but I don't want to pressure you into that."

"I'm not sure what I want you to do for me while we're there, but yes, I'm sure I want you there." *Needed* him was more like it.

"Guess I better get home to pack a bag." He smiled the kind of smile that took loads off a person's back, and I knew instantly I'd made the right decision.

\* \* \* \*

I kept myself together for the rest of the night and through the long flight to the West Coast, never once crying or losing the calm facade I had mastered. Boyd was helpful at every turn. While I wasn't sure what capacity I needed him most in, he maintained the role of assistant, carrying my bags, directing my next moves. Underneath the layers of stress and tension, I was grateful for his presence, which both kept me sane and knocked me a bit off balance. He was so good at doing things for me at the office—I was used to that—but doing things for me that didn't involve work or sex? It was harder to grasp.

After we landed in San Francisco, the awkwardness was lost in busyness. Boyd and I separated, he taking our luggage to the hotel and checking us in while I went straight to the hospital. Even though he still refused to see me, I stayed in the waiting room nearest Ben's unit until visiting hours were over, making sure I checked in with each of his providers and the nurses on duty, explaining what I knew about his medical and mental history to Dr. Evans, verifying that the staff had an accurate representation of his past abuse and depression.

By the end of visiting hours, I was exhausted and hungry and ready to collapse from being awake so long, not to mention the emotional wear of the past day. Boyd, who'd texted me several times, had a cab outside when I left the hospital and dinner waiting for me when I arrived at our hotel room.

As thoughtful as it all was, though, all I wanted to do was sleep. I passed out on top of the bed covers, without taking more than a bite to eat.

When I woke up again, it was dark out. The bedside clock read 4:38. The blankets had been pulled over me—I didn't know how he'd managed that—and Boyd was sleeping in his clothes beside me, as though he'd fallen asleep waiting for me to wake up.

Carefully, so as not to disturb him, I crawled out of bed and went to the bathroom. I guess I wasn't careful enough, though, because when I returned, Boyd was awake, ordering breakfast from room service.

"You need to eat something," he said by way of explanation when he hung up.

"Okay." I *was* pretty hungry. "Thanks." I perched on the edge of the bed, not sure what to do or what to say.

Thankfully, he knew. Handing me the remote for the television, he said, "Here's this if you want some noise. I can get your computer if you want it. Or we can talk. Or I can listen. I can make you a bath. I can take one with you. Whatever you want, it's up to you. Pretend I'm not here, or use me how you need me. Okay?"

"Okay," I said again. I didn't want to talk. And I didn't think I could focus on work. Really, I didn't know what I wanted.

I turned on the TV, settling on the first channel that had something that wasn't an infomercial—some sci-fi show I'd never seen before. We watched in silence.

When our food arrived, we moved to the table, and I picked at my plate, managing to eat half of my omelet before pushing it away.

Then, over a cup of too strong coffee, I opened up—as much as I ever had, anyway, telling Boyd about my childhood, about the father who beat us, about my gay brother who'd taken the brunt of his abuse. I was straightforward and somber, my story concise and undetailed.

Boyd, on the other hand, listened. Listened without judgment, adding commentary only when he needed clarification.

And even though I didn't cry or get emotional, it felt good to finally get it all off my chest. Felt good to finally be *talking* instead of *fixing*. Felt good to be heard.

"So your father is getting out of jail this summer?"

"Yes. Which is fine with me—he doesn't bother me. But for the sake of my siblings, I wish he would stay locked up forever. You better believe I'm doing everything in my power to make that happen."

"I believe it," he said, leaning back in his chair, his arms folded over his chest. "It sounds like you've done a really good job with them. They're lucky to have you."

I nodded in thanks. I was good at that—good at receiving compliments that I didn't agree with. Truth was, one of the reasons I loved being praised so much was because I always secretly feared that I was a failure. That I hadn't done enough. That *I* wasn't enough.

It was a pointless thing to argue, so I usually said thanks and feigned acceptance.

But this time, Boyd wouldn't let me pretend. He sat forward, his expression intense. "I mean it, Norma. You've done a good job."

I rolled my eyes. "I haven't."

"You have."

I let out a cynical laugh. "I haven't. I've done everything wrong. Ben doesn't want to live, and Gwen is too scared to let anyone in, and after thousands spent on the best lawyers in the state, my father's getting out of jail anyway."

"But that's because of flaws in the legal system, not flaws with you. And Ben *does* want to live. He just needs help figuring out how, and you're showing him. And Gwen's still young. She'll change."

"How can you know that?" I didn't bother mentioning that Boyd was younger than my sister.

He shrugged. "I can't. But I can have faith. *You* let *me* in."

Our eyes met, as I thought about what he'd said. *Had* I let him in? When had that happened? Was it just starting now or was this simply the first I was realizing it?

I was still chewing through those thoughts when he asked, "Do you trust me? Do you trust me to give you what you need right now?"

Yeah, I did trust him. Especially to take care of me. Even more especially, to take care of me with sex. So, I softly said, "Yes," held out my hand, and let him lead me to the bed.

He undressed me slowly, intently, paying attention to every detail of the process, kissing each part of my skin as he uncovered it. He caressed me, ran his hands all over my body, then went down on me, giving me the sweetest of orgasms.

Honestly, it hadn't been the most earth-shattering of climaxes—I was probably too distracted and emotionally worn out for that—but it was nice to just feel good for a few minutes.

"Thank you," I said when he came back up to kiss me, my taste fresh on his lips.

He chuckled softly. "That was only the preparation. Turn over."

I was curious but had learned to bite my tongue. I rolled over, exposing my backside, which he massaged thoroughly. I was a puddle by the time he paused to undress, all my muscles limp and lax.

When he was naked, he crawled up behind me. "Bend your knees under you." I followed his directions, raising my ass into the air when he nudged me to do so. He ran his palm over one of my cheeks then slipped his hand down to my cunt where he fucked me with his fingers until I was dripping.

"Good girl. That's what I wanted." He continued to quietly encourage me as he trailed my wetness back toward my other hole.

Automatically, I tensed. We'd talked about ass play before, and I was for it—just, we hadn't actually done anything there yet.

"Relax, baby," Boyd said, circling my rim with the pad of his finger. "Trust me. Rub your clit while I do this, okay?"

I dropped my hand between my legs and began rubbing the swollen nub, careful not to make myself come too soon. Then I closed my eyes and pressed my forehead into the pillow. I took a deep breath and slowly let it out.

As I pushed the air out of my lungs, Boyd pushed his finger inside of me.

"Oh my god." *Oh my god*, it felt so…*good*. So different than I'd ever expected, a million nerves firing with pleasure as he rubbed me. Jesus, if he kept this up, I was going to come. Just from this.

It wasn't long at all before he added a second finger. Then he was pushing in deeper, past the tight ring of muscles, until his fingers were completely buried.

I moaned.

"It feels good, doesn't it?" He stroked in and out of me as he spoke, not really seeming to expect a response, which was good since

I was beyond the capability of forming words. "This would be better if it were my cock right now. You'd get what you really need to release, but I haven't worked you up to that. We'll have to settle for this instead."

Yes, I could settle for this. It felt amazing and new and was really distracting. My head was focused on nothing but this—nothing but him and what he was doing to me.

When I was near orgasm, Boyd changed the game yet again. He positioned his cock at my pussy then shoved in as he pulled his fingers out of my ass. Once he was seated inside me, he drew out of my pussy, pushing his fingers back into my ass again.

Fire. I was on fire. Everywhere electricity shot through my body as he continued to work his cock and fingers in and out of me in opposition like a seesaw. It was like nothing I'd felt before. Spots formed before my eyes, my legs began to shake under me, and I didn't know if I was going to come or cry, but there was something inside me about to let loose. Something big.

And when it did—when my orgasm began to wash over me with huge tsunami-like waves—Boyd pulled me back onto his lap. With one arm wrapped around my breasts, he left his fingers in my ass and drove into me with his cock. God, I'd thought the seesaw motion was intense, and this was all that and more. I felt so full, so incredibly full. Each of his thrusts sent ripples of release like aftershocks, until I was coming and coming and coming with no stop.

And then the tears came.

Not the kind of tears that often burned at my eyes when I climaxed, but torrents. I was sobbing, my body shuddering with the attempt to get it all out.

Immediately, Boyd pulled out of me, twisting so he could embrace me. I clutched onto him, crying into his chest while he rocked me and cooed in my ear. "That's it. Let it out. Let it all out."

I did just that, let out everything that had been pent up inside for the last twenty-four hours. Hell, for the last twenty-four years. For a lifetime.

After I'd finished, I let him hold me, and when my head cleared and my cheeks dried, all I could think about was how much I loved his arms. How much I loved his chest. How much I loved the way he held me. How much I loved him in my life.

Then it occurred to me. "I love you," I said, pulling back to see his face. "Do you know that?"

He seemed pleased, though not all that surprised. "I thought maybe you might." He rubbed his thumb along my cheekbone. "I think you know I love you too."

I hadn't thought about it before, but now that I had, I realized I did know. "You've loved me for quite some time, haven't you?"

He didn't answer in words. He didn't have to. Instead, he kissed me, shifting so that I fell underneath him.

And this time when he made love to me, I realized that's what we'd always done—make love. That just because we'd only said the words now, every time we'd been together before—every time Boyd had instructed me and bossed me and taken me—it had always been *making love.*

I'd known going into my relationship with Boyd that I could never lose him as an assistant. From day one, I'd decided that if it came down to having to choose between transferring him in order to comply with the office rules or giving up our extracurricular romance, I'd pick keeping him at the job. Because that's the type of woman I was, the type I'd always been. My career was my priority. Staying on top in my field came first.

Or it had.

Now, that decision seemed much harder to make, if not impossible. And I was more than certain I'd eventually have to figure it out.

# Chapter Nine

Boyd and I managed to keep the status quo for another year and a half. At work, I had the power, at home, he had the power, and between the two we practiced a satisfactory balance. We still had designated nights that we spent together, but I had so many of my belongings at his place, and he had so many at mine, that I no longer needed to pack a bag. My building manager was on a first name basis with Boyd. His sister invited me to her bachelorette party. We were a totally committed couple to anyone who knew us well enough.

While we stayed steady, the relationships with those close to me changed significantly. Ben fell in love with both life and a boy and moved back to New York. Hudson met someone and got married, and Gwen became best friends with his new bride. Often, we'd gather for dinner parties at the Pierces', and for the first time, there were people that I truly cared about outside of my family. It was a refreshingly happy time.

But, with happiness, I'd become restless.

It had been two years since Boyd first made his move, and as much as I enjoyed the dynamics of our love affair, I hated having to keep so much of it secret. My siblings knew, as did Hudson's wife, but that was all. Particularly, I was frustrated with not being able to invite Boyd to any social gathering where people from work might be present. Such as Hudson. With Gwen's newfound friendship with the Pierces, there weren't many events I was invited to that he wasn't part of.

Funny how, once upon a time, I would have killed to be such a vital part of Hudson's private life. Now, I found it a nuisance.

"You've been quiet tonight. What's up?" Boyd asked one Friday evening in June after one such Pierce party.

We were in his kitchen cleaning up after dinner, and though I did have something I'd been meaning to talk to him about, I wasn't quite sure I was ready. More accurately, I wasn't sure if *we* were ready for where this particular discussion would lead us.

Ever sensitive to me, my hesitation signaled alarms for Boyd. "Norma? Is something wrong?"

"Not wrong, exactly. Just." I finished rinsing off the dish I was holding and handed it to him to put into the dishwasher. "It's sort of funny you should bring this up. I had an interesting conversation with Hudson that I was meaning to tell you about."

"Oh, really?" That was all he said, and with just that and the cock of his brow, he brought out the authoritative Boyd—the Boyd that had full command over me. The Boyd that I answered immediately when questioned.

I leaned my hip against the counter and took a breath before plunging in. "Basically, Hudson knows." That was the easiest way to say it, really. It had been a brief confrontation, but he'd made it clear that he was fully aware of the relationship I had with my subordinate. The very unauthorized relationship.

"Hudson knows?" Another second and Boyd realized what I was getting at. "Ah, he *knows*."

His forehead furrowed, and I knew he was considering the information carefully before responding with more. Silently, he retrieved a bottle of detergent from the cupboard and poured it into the dishwasher.

I chewed my lip as I waited, each quiet second making me more and more tense. It was strange how this moment felt like it had been coming for so long and how now that it was here, I was totally unprepared. Why hadn't we ever talked about what would happen if we were discovered? Why had we never laid out plans for a future? Did Boyd's silence indicate he hadn't given much thought to this possibility? That wasn't like him. He usually had a plan for everything where we were concerned.

I usually had a plan for everything *but* where we were concerned. He'd taught me to rely on him. Now I realized how vulnerable that left me. How much trust I'd put in him.

He didn't speak until he'd started the dishwasher. "Did he come out and say that directly? Did he confront you about it?"

"No, he didn't say it directly, but he made it pretty clear. Good news is that I don't think he's going to make a big deal about it."

"How do you know that? What did you say?" He'd straightened to his full height, and something in his tone prickled with irritation, which automatically made me feel guarded.

"There really wasn't an opportunity to respond," I said, standing straighter myself—as though I could match his height. "He made this insinuating announcement that as long as perception is in check, that's all he cares about."

"*Perception,*" he repeated, and it wasn't a question but more like a confirmation of fact.

"Right. Which I assume means that as long as no one knows then our relationship isn't an issue."

"*Isn't an issue.*" This time his echo had bite to it.

I crossed my arms over my chest. "You don't sound happy."

"I didn't realize I should be happy that what we are to each other is being considered as a possible *issue* by someone who has nothing to do with our relationship." Boyd wiped his hands off with a dishtowel and tossed it angrily onto the counter before moving to the fridge.

"When you put it like that..." I watched as he pulled out a beer and popped the top. If I hadn't known he was frustrated before, I certainly did now—Boyd rarely drank.

*Fuck.*

"Come on," I said, as he took a swig. "It's not that bad, is it? So we have to stay in the closet about our relationship, but at least we don't have to worry about the boss finding out."

He leaned against the counter, his expression sour.

"You're making a face."

"I'm not making any face. I'm processing."

I threw my hands up in the air. "There's nothing to process. What's there to process?"

He answered with another swallow of beer.

Sighing, I went to him. "So Hudson knows. As long as no one else knows, we're cool." I ran a hand up each of his arms, trying to soothe him.

Boyd remained stiff under my touch. "And how long do you think we can manage to keep everyone else in the dark? How many times have we almost been caught?" It was true that there'd been some close calls. "Your sister actually *did* catch us—"

"That was more than a year ago," I said, cutting him off, "and we've been careful in the office since then." She'd walked in on us in my office on my birthday. It had been after hours, and Boyd was entertaining my request for a little role reversal while he delivered some spankings. It had been the best birthday present I'd ever received, but perhaps not the most appropriate location to have acted out the fantasy.

I wrapped my arms around his neck, pressing into him. "We can be even more careful if you're worried."

"What about when we bumped into Chad Long at the theater? The only way we could have avoided that was to not have gone out together. Should we never go on dates in public in case we run into someone from the office?"

"No. I wasn't saying…" I tilted my head to look at him. "What are you getting at? This is what it is. What it's always been."

He took another swig of his beer then set the bottle on the counter next to him. "And because of what it is, we're stuck like this. With no hope of going anywhere else. This is how our relationship stands. Is this all you want?" His eyes searched mine.

"No. It's not. I want more." My voice rasped with the honesty I'd never shared with him. "I want everything with you."

His body relaxed. He wrapped his arms around my waist. "How do you suggest we work that out if we're hiding our relationship from everyone?" His question was serious and pointed, but less harsh than he'd been before. "Secret wedding? Rings we remove every day before we go into the office? We wouldn't even be able to talk about kids, let alone have them."

"Whoa. Hold on." I took a step back, but he held me in place.

"You said you wanted everything. I was simply bringing up what most people label as 'everything.'" He narrowed his eyes, studying me. "Have you not thought about any of this?"

"Of course I have." And I had. Sort of. And also sort of not. As much of a planner as I was, Boyd had trained me to leave the nuts and bolts of our relationship to him. Which didn't mean I hadn't imagined he'd be in my future. "I just…I just hadn't thought through the details of marriage and family. I always assumed that when we finally got to that point, I'd make the sacrifice and lose having you as my assistant."

He dropped his arms from my waist as he let out an incredulous laugh. "*You*'d make the sacrifice?"

It took everything in me not to roll my eyes. "I didn't mean that you wouldn't be affected. Of course you would." But he didn't care about his job like I did. He'd said that from the beginning. He could get a job anywhere. I, on the other hand, would have to give up my right-hand man. "I'm just the one who would lose more."

"Because I'm the one who works for you."

"Right." Something in his expression told me I'd said the wrong thing, but I couldn't for the life of me figure out what it was or how to fix it.

He held his scowl for several seconds. Then he shook his head. "You know what? I don't want to talk about this anymore." He reached for his beer and took another swallow before dumping the rest out in the sink. "I want you naked, kneeling on the floor in the bedroom with your mouth ready."

"Yes, sir." It was a sudden shift of mood on his part, one I wasn't going to argue. I really did want everything with him someday, but I was just as happy to hold on to what we had for as long as possible before demanding more.

\* \* \* \*

Ten minutes later, I was naked, kneeling before him, my hands wrapped around his erection as I teased his head with my lips.

Boyd was still dressed, his briefs and jeans he'd changed into after work pulled down just far enough to give me full access to his cock. Though he didn't ask for me to do it very often, I loved giving him blowjobs. It was one of the few times in our sexual encounters that he allowed me to have some of the control. Giving him what he needed, watching him react without my own pleasure distracting him—it was a big turn-on. I was already wet now, and I'd barely even touched him.

That needed to be remedied.

Flattening my tongue, I sucked his crown into my mouth and peered up at him.

Boyd wrapped his hands in my hair, much like he always did when I blew him, but this time he did something else, something he hadn't done before—he shoved his entire length into my mouth so that his tip hit the back of my throat.

Spit gathered in my mouth as I struggled not to gag, recovering only when he pulled back out. But before I had more than a second to recover, he thrust back in, as deep as before. Deeper. I dropped my hands to my thighs, my fingernails digging into my skin while he pressed my head toward him, forcing me to accept more of him. He held me there briefly then slid out.

This time when he drove back in, I was ready for him. Or more ready for him, and the urge to gag was easier to manage. He developed a rhythm—slow, deep, invasive—and while it was nothing like the playful teasing BJ I normally gave him, it wasn't altogether unpleasant. And it was definitely erotic. Especially when he forced himself all the way inside, so far in that I practically choked.

"You're doing such a good job taking my big cock," he grunted. "I know it's hard to take it all. It's uncomfortable, but you like it anyway, don't you?"

He pulled out enough for me to hum an, "Mmhmm," as he glided back in.

His grip tightened in my hair, and I gasped around him. "Close your mouth," he ordered, and I did, relishing the pleasure-pain, trying to focus on not gagging, on giving Boyd exactly what he wanted. So many balls to juggle. It was work to do this for him, but the expression on his face and the sounds he let out as he rammed into me over and over made every bit of the effort worth it.

He was getting close to coming. I could feel it in the way his balls tightened as he pressed against me. "So good, Norma," he said hoarsely. "You're so good at taking all of me all the way. I know it's not easy, but you like servicing me like this."

God, I *so* did.

"Would you want to serve someone else in this way?"

"Uh-uh," I managed when I realized he expected an answer.

He pulled out then, swiftly and suddenly. Bending down, he jerked my head back to meet his eyes. "And that's how I feel about my job. It might be hard, it might be menial, but I love doing it *for you*. I don't want to do it for someone else."

With a groan of frustration, he let go of my hair and stormed out of the room.

I was too stunned to call after him. Too stunned to move. And as the meaning of what he'd said sank in, I was also too embarrassed.

Ugh. How narrow-minded was I to think I was the only one who'd lose something if he didn't work for me anymore? I never wanted to leave Pierce Industries, but I had enough autonomy and respect in my field I could easily get another management position that would afford me the same comforts no matter whom I reported to. A job like Boyd's, where the main task was to basically serve someone else all day long? Yeah, who his boss was probably mattered even more than who mine was.

I gave it a couple of minutes before I padded out of the room after him. I found him standing over the kitchen sink, drinking a glass of water. He knew I was there—I hadn't been quiet, and his back tensed as I approached him.

Pressing my body against him, I wrapped my arms around his chest and said quietly, "I'm sorry. I'm dumb and self-centered."

He sighed. "You're not either of those things."

"I am. I didn't think."

He set his glass in the sink but didn't turn around. "It's not like I don't know that he holds the cards here. It's his decision. There's only so much you can do."

My chest twisted inside. While I was sure I'd proven that I didn't still have feelings for the man, it hadn't occurred to me that Hudson still had a power over me that might make Boyd jealous.

It wasn't right. If I loved him more than anyone—more than *anything*—then I had to be willing to give things up in order to ensure a future together. "I could do more to push things. And I haven't. I want to, though."

He glanced over his shoulder. "You do?"

"I do." I stepped back to let him turn toward me. Then I let him pull me into his arms.

"What are you thinking you should do?"

"I don't know exactly. I just know that you're my priority. I want my life to reflect that."

*Even if that means I have to give up my job?*

The question was in the air even though neither of us had spoken it.

I wasn't ready to think about that. "I want those things, Boyd, but I need some more time. Can I have that? Time to sort through our options. Together. Can you give me that?"

His embrace tightened around me. "I'll give you forever, Norma. Because I want everything with you too. But the stuff we do in private? This structure between us that no one else sees is not the only significant part of our relationship. What happens in the office where you're in charge is just as important. Asking me to give that up is as detrimental to the balance of what we have as if I were to ask you to give up what we have in our alone time."

"I get it. Now. And I agree."

He stroked a hand through my hair, as soft and tender as it was hard when he'd gripped it earlier. "I understand that things might have to change in ways we don't want, that we might have to make concessions to set up what we both need, but there has to be some semblance of what we have now in whatever life we settle on. If it takes time to get that, I'm willing to wait."

A small bubble of panic pressed against my ribs but quickly dissolved. In another life it would have grown. In that life, nothing took the place of my ambition and drive to be at the top of every corporate ladder I was allowed to climb.

In this life, though, I'd learned the beauty in not always being the one on top. I'd learned the pleasure of being under too.

Standing on my tiptoes, I reached up to kiss the man who'd taught me that life-changing lesson. Though I started it, he quickly took over, sliding his tongue against mine with sultry strokes that soon had me wet and trembling and aware that I was still very much naked.

"I really do love you," I said when he pulled away, both of us out of breath.

He pressed one more kiss on my nose then spanked my ass with a sharp *thwack*. "Then get back to the bedroom. I'm going to make you prove how much."

# Chapter Ten

*Five Months Later*
*November*

After that, Boyd and I maintained the perception that Hudson desired, but everything was different. Though we still went through the routine we'd gone through for the past two years and still lived the roles we'd defined for ourselves, we'd reached a new understanding between us. We talked about our future a lot. It was our priority, and things began to change. Gwen got a place of her own, and Boyd officially gave up his apartment and moved in with me. He accompanied me to family dinners—even when Hudson was present. And little by little, I started tidying up projects at work so that I could hand them off to someone else if necessary.

Still, time went by. Thanksgiving came and went. The Monday after the four-day holiday, the annual executive Christmas party invitation arrived via intra-office mail.

"You can toss that," I said to Boyd as he laid it on my desk.

"You aren't planning to go? It's at American Cut. Hudson's rented out the entire restaurant. You love that place."

I looked up from my computer screen. "I know. But it's not as fun when I can't take whom I want to take." The year before I'd gone to the event and barely lasted an hour before I'd rushed home to Boyd and had a very different kind of party.

The corners of his mouth bent into a frown. Quietly, so no one passing by might hear, he said, "I hate that I'm the one standing in the way of you enjoying all the perks of your hard work."

"It's not really a perk. It's one night. I'll live." But, the truth was, it was more than one night. My job required me to attend several events throughout the year. Time and time again I'd gone alone. I could ignore the looks and office gossip about my perpetually single status, but I despised not being able to share those occasions with Boyd. Sometimes I'd take him with me as my assistant, which was almost worse. At least at the office, I had work to distract me from pining for his glance or his touch. In social settings, it had gotten harder and harder not to brush my arm against his too closely, not to reach for his hand, not to behave too familiarly with him.

"Okay, then. If that's what you want." Boyd reached for the invitation, but I placed my hand on his wrist to stop him.

"You know what? It's not what I want. And I'm tired of living like this." I pushed my chair back from my desk and stood up.

With the invitation firmly in my grasp, I marched out of my office and down the hallway to Hudson's office. Boyd followed on my heels, and though I could palpably feel his curiosity, he didn't ask any questions.

Hudson's office door was open when I got there, and when I peeked in over his secretary's shoulder, I could see him talking on his phone. "I need a moment of his time," I told her.

"He's just finishing up a call." She looked down at her telephone console, and as she did, the red light indicating Hudson's line went dark. "Oh, there. He's off. Let me announce—"

"Stay here," I said to Boyd before she could finish then walked off before she could stop me. As I walked to his desk, I heard her voice over his speaker. "Norma Anders is here to see you."

"I'd ask you to send her in," Hudson said into the intercom, "but I see there's no need. Thank you, Patricia." His finger left the button before she could respond. "Norma. Please, have a seat."

"I'll stand, thank you."

His eyes darted from me back to the doorway, where I could see Boyd chatting with Trish, then back again. "All right. What can I do for you, then?"

It wasn't unusual for me to meet with Hudson several times in a day, but it was generally always with an appointment and usually when Boyd accompanied me, he came into the actual room. Hudson had to sense something was up.

And something was.

I set the party invitation in front of him. "I'd like to attend this," I said, tapping the card.

"Excellent. You can RSVP with Patri—"

"And I'm bringing Boyd. As my date," I added, before he assumed that I meant anything else.

Hudson cocked a stern brow. "We've talked about this before. I thought you understood my position."

"We have. And I do understand your position. You, however, do not understand mine." I widened my stance and stood up even straighter. "Boyd and I are not a random office fling. We are not a relationship that is going to run its course. We've been together for two and a half years, and we are past the point of sneaking around. We're ready to make a permanent life together, and the one thing standing in our way is you. This job."

Hudson opened his mouth, but I cut him off with a single finger in the air, indicating that I wasn't ready for him to speak.

"Before you suggest it, I am not interested in transferring him to another office. I don't want another assistant, and he doesn't want to work for someone else. We've developed a stellar working relationship that has taken several years to cultivate. It would behoove all of us—you, especially—to keep that relationship intact. The hours required to train a new employee would be a waste of my skill and energy. I'm sure you'd agree that time would much be better suited serving you in other ways."

"Of course, but there are—"

I interrupted him, guessing the possible end of his statement. "I'm sure there are other people who could do the job as well or better, and I'm sure there are reasons that you have this policy in place, but frankly, I don't give a damn anymore. I want Boyd. He's the best assistant I've ever had, and I don't see how my personal relationship with him affects that. We've obviously proven we can remain professional."

Hudson pursed his lips. He'd called me a tiger before, but this was the first time I could remember using my prowess on him. If it threw him for a loop, he didn't show any indication. The man had a poker face that could win national championships.

"Are you asking for something specific, Norma?" he asked after a beat.

I didn't even blink. "Yes. I'm asking for you to let us see each other openly."

He considered, and for half a second I could remember what I'd once seen in him. This power he held was so intoxicating, so seductive, yet, here in the business world, I didn't like it used against me—I wanted to be the one wielding it. How had I ever thought he'd be the right man for me? Funny, how clearly I could see he wasn't now.

And with that authority I envied, he said, "I'm sure you realize that if I'm lax on the fraternization policy with one of my employees, then I'll have to be lax with others. There are very good reasons the rule is in place. It's the best protection we've found against sexual harassment lawsuits. It's a very standard policy."

Nothing he said was news. It also wasn't a deterrent—not today. "I understand completely. I'm telling you to find a loophole. I've been a damned good employee. I've given you years. I've asked for very few favors. I've been loyal. Now show me you're loyal too."

The slight twitch of his eyelid told me I'd hit a nerve. "I'm very appreciative of your loyalty, Norma. This has nothing to do with that. I'm not sure there's any way around this, not with the conditions you're requiring."

"Then you'll have to find another chief financial advisor. Your 'no' should be considered synonymous with my resignation, effective January first." The words were out of my mouth before I had time to stop them. Luckily, I didn't want to.

Hudson leaned back in his chair. "Tough terms you've got there."

"I've learned from the best." I could feel my pulse thrumming in my veins as I waited for him to say more. Could hear the buzz of the fan in his computer and the tap-tap-tap of Trish typing in the reception area behind me. Could sense Boyd's ears pricked to hear our conversation.

Several long seconds passed. Finally, Hudson said, "I'll consider it."

"That's all?" After all the buildup, I was dying for a resolution. How could he leave me hanging?

"For now, yes."

My eyes widened, my mouth opening and shutting as I searched for something else to say, something that would convince him I meant business. Something to convince him to give me his decision right the fuck now. "One way or another, he's coming with me to that party, Hudson."

"Then I'll give you my answer before then. Now if that'll be all..." He picked up his phone as though he meant to make another call.

A little miffed to be so curtly dismissed, I paused. But I'd said what I'd come to say, and that was Hudson's way, after all. "Yes. That's it." Then I spun around and left.

Boyd and I didn't say a word as we walked down the hall toward my office. I was pretty sure he'd heard my discussion with Hudson, but he'd given no indication or reaction, and each step that we took in silence, the pounding of my heart in my ears got louder and my breaths got shallower.

*Oh my god.*

What had I done?

Boyd followed me into my office and closed the door, then pressed his back against it, and for half a second I thought, *keep the door open, you fool! Someone will spread rumors!*

And then it hit me—rumors didn't matter anymore. After what I'd just said? After what I'd told Hudson? It didn't matter what anyone else thought because Boyd and I were about to come out of the closet.

Too agitated to sit down, I paced the room a few times then stopped and turned toward Boyd.

He smiled as I met his stare. "You're hot."

I *was* hot. Like, sweating hot. My hands were clammy, and I was sure my face was red. I started pacing again, fanning myself. "I have so much adrenaline right now. That felt good."

Boyd crossed his arms over his chest. "You know that threats like that only work if you're prepared to follow through with them."

That was the problem. Or it wasn't a problem because, even though I'd acted on impulse, I was determined to stand behind my actions. "I am totally prepared to follow through."

*Wait! Fuck.* I froze as realization came tumbling over me. "I should have talked to you about it first! What was I thinking?"

"We've *been* talking about it. This is your court, remember? I trust you here." Every note of his tone said he was sincere. My skin tingled with the acknowledgment of his faith. It was a good thing we had, Boyd and I, where he could lead me and rule me so masterfully at times and then so easily bend to my wishes at others.

"Thank you," I said quietly, and I hoped he understood all that I was expressing gratitude for.

His wink said he did.

"I'm just surprised," he added. "You'd really leave Pierce Industries?"

"Why not?" I shrugged, a giddy grin on my lips. My body twitched with excitement and nerves, and I had to pace again to have a place to direct the energy. "There are a hundred different companies that would clamor for me. I'd include in my hiring requirements that I bring my own assistant and make sure there are no corporate policies banning fraternization among superiors and their subordinates. It could be a whole new beginning."

His eyes narrowed into dark pools. "You're giving me such wicked fantasies about the kinds of fraternizing we could arrange."

"Be good." I pointed a stern finger in case he was considering not being good. Honestly, I wouldn't have required much convincing to join him in wickedness, but nothing about our relationship was official yet. I had to keep up pretenses.

Boyd cocked his head, his gaze searching. "You love it here, Norma. You live for this place." I could hear what he was really asking—*are you sure? You don't have to do this if you're not.*

But I was surer than I'd been in a long time. "I do love it here. I've built my whole career on this company. I'd be very sad to have to go. But I can live without anything except you."

He held my gaze from across the room, and even though he didn't need to say the words, he did. "I love you."

I breathed it in, let his love settle in my bones.

Then, in mock Hudson fashion, I dismissed him. "Get to work."

"Yes, boss."

* * * *

Two weeks later, Hudson still hadn't given me a response, and the Christmas party was only days away. I'd expected that as the time approached I'd have second thoughts about leaving, and it had crossed my mind to give Hudson a little longer to figure things out. It was the holiday season, after all.

But, really, I didn't want to wait. I was ready. Not to leave my job, but ready to present Boyd as my other half. Every minute that passed, I was more excited about that than I was worried about what would happen in my career. I was actually surprised I'd been able to live so long with our relationship a secret.

It was him I was thinking about when we met that Monday morning in conference room B for the weekly financials meeting. He was sitting right next to me, as he always did, taking notes as Hudson spoke, marking things on my calendar.

Usually I was an active participant at these things. Today, perhaps because I was already pulling away in my mind, I was quiet, remembering instead the first time that Boyd had shown me his other side. It had been here, in this very room, my body stretched across this table. If I closed my eyes, I could almost feel it, as if it were happening now. His breath on my thighs, the brush of his fingers on my pussy…

A sharp jab of his elbow in my upper arm brought my attention back to the meeting. I glanced at Boyd, who, with his eyes, gestured for me to focus on Hudson.

"…precedence to change the current corporate policy," Hudson was saying.

My brow furrowed as I tried to catch up.

"My wife manages The Sky Launch nightclub," he went on, "a company owned, for all intents and purposes, by Pierce Industries. While it might be a distant enough working relationship to be considered a moot point, I can see several situations where she might be hired on to work directly beneath me. In order to circumvent any issues that might arise from that, I'm amending the present fraternization standards."

*Wait. What?*

I didn't move, yet it felt like I was in the movies where

everything all of a sudden went fuzzy except the people pertinent to the plot. The entire room full of peers and their assistants disappeared, and the only people left were Boyd and me, and this life-changing decree from Hudson.

"Dating among supervisors and subordinates will still be disallowed to protect the company from sexual harassment lawsuits," Hudson said, not even looking at me but addressing me all the same. "However, there will be no violation if the couple is married."

Under the table, where no one could see, Boyd grabbed my hand with his and squeezed.

Hudson went on with his announcement, unimportant words and phrases that skated past me. I didn't care what else he had to say—he'd found a way for Boyd and me to be together and still keep our current working arrangement. It was all I could do not to jump up from my seat and kiss him. Or, more tempting, kiss Boyd.

Something about the way Boyd's fingers linked with mine told me there would be plenty of kissing later on.

It seemed like forever before Hudson wrapped things up. Finally, he said, "If there are any questions on this change, you can contact Bernie in Human Resources. Otherwise, the new policy will go out in formal documentation through an intra-office e-mail later this week." He stood. "Meeting adjourned."

Neither Boyd nor I moved while the room cleared out, our hands still laced under the table. When there were only a few stragglers, deep in their own conversation, I turned to Boyd, unable to hold it in another second. "Civil ceremony?"

His eyes danced with as much eagerness as mine. "We can follow up with something more formal later for friends and family. A small event in the Hamptons, perhaps."

"We only have five days until the Christmas party."

He shook his head, as though he'd already thought of that and had it under control. "I'll start working on the arrangements as soon as we get back to the office. You have a couple hours free on Friday afternoon. I'm thinking that could work."

Damn. I'd be married by the weekend. And I wouldn't have to quit my job. And Boyd wouldn't have to transfer. And he could continue being the perfect assistant and lover and, soon, husband!

My vision clouded with excited tears. "Does this mean that we're officially engaged?"

With a ridiculously happy grin, Boyd nodded. "I guess it solves the problem of who's going to propose."

I tightened my grip on his hand. "Oh, it was always going to be me."

# Epilogue

I hired another assistant a year later.

Chelsea is a redheaded spitball of personality with excellent organization skills and dynamic interpersonal relations.

She's definitely no Boyd, and thankfully, Chelsea only had to cover for him for three months while he took a leave in order to be home to help our foster daughter get settled. Kira is a dark-skinned, three-year-old girl with a soft voice and big smile, despite the burns left on her face and arms from her abusive, meth-addicted biological mother. We're in the process of adopting her, but she's already ours in every way but blood.

Now that she's used to her new routine, Boyd works in the office for four hours a day while Kira's at preschool. Then he rushes out to pick her up and take her to therapy and play group and just be a parent that's there for her. *Mr. Mom*, I call him, which always earns me a spanking or two, so I'll never stop.

"I didn't finish typing up Norma's agenda for the conference next week," I hear Boyd say today as Chelsea comes in to take the afternoon shift. "Can you finish that and then get her presentation ready?" Yep, still the best assistant ever. Always taking care of me.

I stand from my desk and walk to the office door. Usually Boyd picks up Kira from school, but today, my brother Ben picked her up and took her out for a mini-uncle/niece outing. He must have texted that he's on his way up if Boyd's now getting ready to leave.

Sure enough, not two minutes have passed when Ben arrives with my squirmy little girl.

"Momma!" Kira says, reaching for me.

"How's my angel?" I say, lifting her for a hug. She's a beautiful, strong girl with a long road ahead of her. The scars on her skin are only half her battle. The worst are the ones on the inside, but my siblings and I are both proof that those can be overcome.

"I had I scream," she says, tugging on my hair, and it's so cute I can't correct her.

"Did you? It looks like you're *wearing* ice cream." I glare at my brother, who shrugs. It was a lighthearted glare, anyway. Clothes can be washed.

I spend a few minutes catching up with my brother until Boyd and Chelsea remind me simultaneously, "It's almost time for your one o'clock meeting."

"Jinx," Chelsea says.

"Momma has to get back to work," I tell Kira. "But if you're a good girl for Daddy, we can have story time when I get home. Okay?" I give her a big hug then wait for Boyd to finish buttoning his coat before I hand her over.

"I'll walk you down," Boyd tells Ben, then presses a kiss to my cheek. "See you tonight, Mrs. Anders-Barrett. Don't work too late."

"Or else...?" I ask playfully.

He leans in so only I can hear. "If you want to be punished for something, I can punish you. You don't have to be late for that to be arranged."

"I'll leave on time," I promise.

He starts to walk away, but I grab his hand to stop him. "What?" he asks.

And, at first, I just shake my head because I can't speak. Because sometimes I get too full of emotion when I think about where I came from and how I got here—when I think about the person I thought I was and the person that Boyd taught me I could be. When I think about how the people I love most—my siblings, my husband, my child—have all found ways to not just survive, but be happy. Have shown *me* how to be happy. It's a lot. A wonderful lot.

Boyd is still staring at me, waiting for me to say something, so I swallow past the lump in my throat. "I was just thinking how lucky I am to have you. That's all."

"I can't say I disagree," he teases.

I reach up to give him a chaste kiss on the lips—just because everyone knows that we're married doesn't mean we shouldn't act appropriately. In public, anyway.

Then this time I let him leave. I have work to do, as always. It's a busy job being a woman at the top, and as they say, lonely. But only if you insist on *always* being on top.

I'm one of the lucky ones who's learned sometimes it's better being underneath.

Sign up for the 1001 Dark Nights Newsletter
and be entered to win a Tiffany Key necklace.

There's a contest every month!

Go to www.1001DarkNights.com to subscribe.

As a bonus, all subscribers will receive a free
1001 Dark Nights story
The First Night
by Lexi Blake & M.J. Rose

Turn the page for a full list of the
1001 Dark Nights fabulous novellas...

# Discover 1001 Dark Nights Collection Three

HIDDEN INK by Carrie Ann Ryan
A Montgomery Ink Novella

BLOOD ON THE BAYOU by Heather Graham
A Cafferty & Quinn Novella

SEARCHING FOR MINE by Jennifer Probst
A Searching For Novella

DANCE OF DESIRE by Christopher Rice

ROUGH RHYTHM by Tessa Bailey
A Made In Jersey Novella

DEVOTED by Lexi Blake
A Masters and Mercenaries Novella

Z by Larissa Ione
A Demonica Underworld Novella

FALLING UNDER YOU by Laurelin Paige
A Fixed Trilogy Novella

EASY FOR KEEPS by Kristen Proby
A Boudreaux Novella

UNCHAINED by Elisabeth Naughton
An Eternal Guardians Novella

HARD TO SERVE by Laura Kaye
A Hard Ink Novella

DRAGON FEVER by Donna Grant
A Dark Kings Novella

KAYDEN/SIMON by Alexandra Ivy/Laura Wright
A Bayou Heat Novella

STRUNG UP by Lorelei James
A Blacktop Cowboys® Novella

MIDNIGHT UNTAMED by Lara Adrian
A Midnight Breed Novella

TRICKED by Rebecca Zanetti
A Dark Protectors Novella

DIRTY WICKED by Shayla Black
A Wicked Lovers Novella

A SEDUCTIVE INVITATION by Lauren Blakely
A Seductive Nights New York Novella

SWEET SURRENDER by Liliana Hart
A MacKenzie Family Novella

*Visit www.1001DarkNights.com for more information.*

# Discover 1001 Dark Nights Collection One

Also from 1001 Dark Nights

*Visit www.1001DarkNights.com for more information.*

# Discover 1001 Dark Nights Collection Two

WICKED WOLF by Carrie Ann Ryan
WHEN IRISH EYES ARE HAUNTING by Heather Graham
EASY WITH YOU by Kristen Proby
MASTER OF FREEDOM by Cherise Sinclair
CARESS OF PLEASURE by Julie Kenner
ADORED by Lexi Blake
HADES by Larissa Ione
RAVAGED by Elisabeth Naughton
DREAM OF YOU by Jennifer L. Armentrout
STRIPPED DOWN by Lorelei James
RAGE/KILLIAN by Alexandra Ivy/Laura Wright
DRAGON KING by Donna Grant
PURE WICKED by Shayla Black
HARD AS STEEL by Laura Kaye
STROKE OF MIDNIGHT by Lara Adrian
ALL HALLOWS EVE by Heather Graham
KISS THE FLAME by Christopher Rice
DARING HER LOVE by Melissa Foster
TEASED by Rebecca Zanetti
THE PROMISE OF SURRENDER by Liliana Hart

Also from 1001 Dark Nights

THE SURRENDER GATE By Christopher Rice
SERVICING THE TARGET By Cherise Sinclair

*Visit www.1001DarkNights.com for more information.*

# About Laurelin Paige

With over 1 million books sold, Laurelin Paige is the *NY Times*, *Wall Street Journal*, and *USA Today* Bestselling Author of the Fixed Trilogy. She's a sucker for a good romance and gets giddy anytime there's kissing, much to the embarrassment of her three daughters. Her husband doesn't seem to complain, however. When she isn't reading or writing sexy stories, she's probably singing, watching *Game of Thrones* and the *Walking Dead*, or dreaming of Michael Fassbender. She's also a proud member of Mensa International though she doesn't do anything with the organization except use it as material for her bio.

You can connect with Laurelin on Facebook at www.facebook.com/LaurelinPaige or on twitter @laurelinpaige. You can also visit her website, www.laurelinpaige.com, to sign up for e-mails about new releases.

# Chandler

A Fixed Trilogy Series Spinoff
By Laurelin Paige
Coming September 20, 2016

From the *New York Times* Bestselling author of The Fixed Trilogy and Hudson…

I dominate the boardroom. I'm a Pierce—it's what we do. But I never had a reason to bring that persona into the bedroom.

Until Genevive Fasbender.

She's brash and bold and stubborn as hell, and she doesn't believe it's possible to satisfy her. But I've discovered her secret, one she hasn't even figured out herself—she wants what I want.

And not only does she want it—I'll make her need it.

No matter what.

\* \* \* \*

*Chandler is a standalone novel, set in the Fixed Trilogy universe. While characters from the Fixed Trilogy and Found Duet will be seen in this story, it is not necessary to have read them to enjoy Chandler.*

"Can you manage to keep your dick in your pants for one night?"

Hudson's question is meant to grab my attention, and it does. To be fair, I heard most of what he'd said up to this point. The parts that were of interest, anyway.

Okay, maybe that wasn't much.

"Probably not. I don't sleep in my pants, for one, and I do plan on sleeping." I pull next to the valet podium at the Whitney Museum of Art, and add, "eventually," because I know it will rile my brother up.

His sigh is heavy with exasperation. "Can you keep your dick in your pants *at the gala?*"

I grab my phone from its dock, automatically switching it out of

Bluetooth mode, and bring it up to my ear. I pretend to consider as I step out of the car and button my tux jacket. "Hmm."

"Nice wheels," the valet says, unconcerned that I'm on the phone.

I pull out my wallet and flash a fifty-dollar bill. "Take care of her and this is yours."

"Yes sir, Mr. Pierce."

If Hudson were here, he'd wince at the recognition. It's possible the valet knows me from the latest list of "Richest Men Under Thirty"—it's the first year I've hit since I only got my trust fund when I turned twenty-four a few months back. But one look at the tattooed, pony-tailed Italian says he isn't the type to read *Forbes*, which means he recognizes me from the gossip sites instead. Honestly, I don't mind that I have a rep. It's the elder Pierce who seems to care.

Speaking of the elder Pierce...

"Can I keep it in my pants until after the gala?" I repeat his earlier question as I stride toward the entrance of the museum. "I don't know. How long is this thing supposed to last?" I'm messing with Hudson. It's too easy not to. And really, what does he expect me to say? It's not like I'm planning to try to get a girl to blow me on the event premises.

Though, if one were to offer...

"And don't hit on anyone while you're there, either."

Now he's going too far. "Is that a baby crying?" I don't really hear a baby crying, but the likelihood that there is one somewhere near him isn't too slim. The recent birth of his twins is the whole reason I'm stuck going to this stupid shindig in the first place.

"I mean it, Chandler."

As if on cue, a baby actually *does* start crying in the background. "Shouldn't you go put a pacifier in it or something?"

Hudson ignores me. "This is an important event," he chides. "Accelecom is about to strike a deal with Werner Media, and it's crucial we make a good impression."

"Yeah, yeah, yeah." It's not like I don't know this. He's told me seventeen times just today, plus several hundred times earlier this week. In fact, every conversation we've had in the past few days has been about Accelecom's charity gala tonight, which is more than a little strange, even for my work-obsessed older brother. Mainly because Werner Media isn't a company we own. Sure, it belongs to family friends, but the Pierces haven't been that close to the Werners since, well, around the time I graduated from high school. So why the fuck does he care so much about the impression I leave?

It suddenly occurs to me to ask. "What exactly is it you hope to gain from my presence here tonight? The Werner-Accelecom merger has nothing to do with Pierce Industries, does it?"

A beat goes by. "It's a good opportunity for you," he says finally. "There will be a lot of press there this evening, and if you play nice, you could get a good write-up, one that doesn't involve the mayor's daughter."

His answer is irritating. Though he's easing me into the family business, I'm technically an owner of Pierce Industries, just like he is, and I hate it when he treats me like an average employee.

But I'm not in the mood to argue.

I'm in the mood to deflect. "Man, that kid of yours is really howling. I didn't know you subscribed to the cry-it-out method. I knew you were old, but 1990's parenting? Come on."

"Chandler." Hudson's tone is clipped and stern. He means it to be intimidating.

Spoiler: Hudson doesn't scare me.

"I'm hanging up now," I say, pushing through the doors of the museum.

"Do you understand what I'm saying?"

"Yes. I understand. *Dad.*"

I expect him to growl about my latest poke, but he's distracted. "I'll take him," I hear him say, his words muffled as though he has his hand over the mouthpiece. Then, more clearly, "Chandler, I have to help Alayna with the babies."

"Finally. Wouldn't want to have to accuse you of child neglect." Without saying goodbye, I click *END* and, after putting it on silent, slip my phone into my inside jacket pocket. Hudson's children can only preoccupy him for so long. Sooner or later, he'll be back to riding my ass, and even though I'm here at this event in his place, as far as I'm concerned, I'm off the clock.

\* \* \* \*

The thing is, Hudson's concerns are somewhat legit. Not because I *can't* keep my cock in my pants, but because most of the time I don't *want* to.

What can I say? I'm a guy who loves women.

Lucky for me, women usually love me too. And why wouldn't they? I'm charming, young, good-looking, smart. Decent at my job, despite what Hudson tells anyone. Oh, and let's not forget, filthy rich. I'm shower masturbation material come to life.

Most impressive, though, is my bedroom portfolio—it's not a secret that I'm a giver. Swear on the Pierce family name, I do not let a woman leave my sheets before she's received at least two orgasms. The goal is always three, but I'm willing to concede that there are sometimes other factors besides me contributing to that outcome. Maybe she's tired. Maybe her head's too into it. Maybe she's not good at relaxing. Whatever, I get it. But she's getting two O's regardless.

Before I start sounding too noble, let me clarify—the orgasms are for *me*. There's nothing like the feel of a pussy clenching around your cock, milking you to your own climax—that's got to be the best definition of heaven around.

But the biggest reason I deliver is because of the cost-benefit ratio. I'm a firm believer in *what goes around, comes around*. The happier she is, the happier she'll want to make me. I'm talking Happy with a capital "H." And while I'm a one-night-only kind of guy—a fact I always make clear from the beginning—I've done really well with referrals. Call it a successful "business" model.

Sometimes *too* successful, considering the way some of the ladies are eyeing me as I glance around the museum.

It only takes one sweep of my gaze to know tonight is not going to create any problems for my brother. The room is filled with the kinds of women I'm one hundred percent not attracted to. Trophy wives looking for a distraction. Cougars who sit on the boards—and the faces—of whatever-and-whoever-is-*in*-this-week. Rich dames with so much Botox and spandex their bodies don't even jiggle when they're supposed to—and if she's lying underneath me, it's supposed to.

That just leaves the women I've already been with, and I don't do repeats.

Well then, let's make this trip an easy in and out, just like I like it. This time when I glance around, I look for the quickest opportunities to achieve the "make a good impression" edict that Hudson has given me. I make a plan. Mingle with the execs from my father's country club, say hello to Warren Werner who I've just spotted by the fondue station, and then put in a bid at the auction in the adjoining room to make sure the Pierce presence is duly noticed.

But first, I need a drink.

A waitress passes by with a tray of caviar. "Excuse me. Is there a bar somewhere?"

She tilts her lip into a flirtatious grin as she checks me out. Now this woman might be an option...

But she's working, and I'll have to stick around until she gets off before I'll have any chance of getting off myself, and I can already tell this thing is going to be a snooze-fest.

Especially when she answers. "There's champagne floating around. And some punch that should be spiked if it hasn't been already."

"Well, shit. I should have brought my flask." Though, if I had, it would have been filled with a single-malt Scotch and not something I'd ever mix, let alone with fruit punch. I wink. "But thanks for the heads-up."

I can tell she wouldn't mind more cozy conversation, but I slip away before she gets any ideas, and after a quick chat with some men I've done business with in the past, I run smack into Warren.

"Chandler! I didn't expect to see you here tonight. Where's Hudson?" The man is practically a father to me, or rather, he was around while I was growing up about as much as my own dad was, which is to say, not much. In other words, I have to talk to him, but it's going to be boring as hell.

I put on my friendliest grin. "Alayna had her babies early. He's taking some time 'off.'" I use air quotes around the word *off* because Warren and I both know my brother works in his sleep.

"Oh, yes. I recall hearing that." He goes on to deliver heartfelt congratulations and the like before moving to the obligatory inquiries about the rest of my family, which I give, dutifully.

This kind of small talk is the worst. I'm dying inside with every polite word. I only manage to tolerate it by dreaming about the real drink I'll get later at The Sky Launch or another one of the nightclubs where hooking up is practically an item on the drink menu.

Eventually, after Warren's told me all about his upcoming plans to retire, I courteously ask about his daughter, Celia—Hudson's childhood peer/possible lover/almost-baby-mama/part-of-a-complicated-friendship-that-I've-never-understood.

Though Warren's expression remains warm, his eyes harden, and I sense he'd prefer not to talk about her with me. While I was too young to be privy to the rift that happened between our once-close families, I have a feeling most of the bad blood has to do with Hudson not marrying Warren's daughter.

"Celia's good," he says curtly. "She's in town at the moment. In fact, she was supposed to be here tonight but ended up canceling because of a headache." *Or because she was afraid she'd run into Hudson.* "You know she's married now to—"

His sentence is cut off by a younger gentleman tapping on his shoulder. "Sorry to interrupt, but Mr. Fasbender is looking for you."

*Fasbender.* I recognize that name. He's the owner of Accelecom and probably one of the people that Hudson would most prefer I be seen with tonight.

Which is why I decide not to bother. I've done a fair bit of schmoozing already. If Hudson wanted more from me, he could have been more specific when he asked. Besides, he needs to learn to deal with disappointment, and who better to teach him but me.

Grabbing a glass of champagne from a passing waiter, I head to the area where the silent auction has been situated. I peruse the items up for bid, quickly bypassing the most popular draws—a houseboat, a vineyard in France, a private island off of Malta—and settle on the gaudiest piece of art I've ever set my eyes on. Complete with a five-inch thick ostentatious gold frame, the six-foot square canvas is covered with abstract red-hued phallic brush strokes. It's bold and brusque. It makes me angry just to look at it.

It's perfect.

I pull a Montblanc fountain pen from my breast pocket and find the next blank line on the auction sheet. Tripling the last amount offered, I fill in my own bid. Then, with a gleeful smirk, I sign Hudson's name and his office phone number before tucking the pen back in my jacket.

There. I'll pose for a picture at the door on my way out for good measure, but otherwise my work here is done. And without causing any trouble. *Consider it a baby gift, Hudson.*

Downing the too-sweet champagne, I turn to search for a place to set my empty glass before making my trek back across the museum floor.

That's when I see her.

My breath is knocked from my chest the second my gaze slams into her. I swear there's a spotlight on her. Cliché, isn't it? But I pull my eyes up toward the ceiling to see if there's a fixture directed at her and am surprised when I find none. Because she literally *shines.*

Frozen to my spot, I ignore the people pressing past me coming to and from the auction tables, drinking in every detail I can of the beauty across the room. Her long shapely legs, her lusciously curved hips, her pouty mouth drawn into a tight line. She's wearing a lace shift dress—my sister owns a boutique, I know these terms—simple in shape, but the pattern is elegant, making her look classier than many of the older women here in their skin-tight bling-bling gowns. She's on the tall side, but not too tall. With her modest heels, she's just the right height to kiss. Just the right height to devour without having to bend. Just the right height to be able to look in her eyes as my hand presses gently at her throat.

Jesus, did I just fantasize about choking a woman? What the fuck is wrong with me? I'm the first to admit I'm a pig, but I've never had those kinds of kinky thoughts. I've never not been a gentleman. Never wanted to not be *nice* like I want to not be nice looking at her. She's just so…captivating.

I'm not the only one who notices. She's surrounded by a flock of men who are not very good at hiding their eagerness to see what's beneath her dress, and I can't say that I blame them. She's *that* alluring. That *hypnotizing.*

She's not even the kind of girl I'm attracted to. Too thin, too brunette. Too young—she can't be more than twenty-five. But there's *something* about her. Something that separates her from the crowd. Something in her gestures as she patiently tolerates her would-be suitors. Something about her posture, which is polished, but aloof. Something about her entire being that keeps my eyes pinned to her like a lion's pinned to his prey.

I should leave. I know this. It's not my M.O. to stalk. I prefer to be the one reeled in—again, part of the model I've successfully honed. But I'm stuck, glued to the spot, staring at this intriguing creature with graceful movements and delicate features.

And then there's a clearing in her swarm of admirers, and I'm suddenly not stuck, but moving toward her, drawn as if on the descent of a zip-line. She hasn't noticed me, and I take advantage of that, circling around her so that I can approach her from behind. It gives me a chance to check her hand when I'm near enough for signs of a ring. A ring is a deal-breaker for me. I don't do infidelity, never have. Once, I came close. Or rather, the situation *felt* close to cheating, and it was terrible. I won't do that again.

But that was five long years ago now and not only has that lesson been learned, it also seems to be unnecessary tonight. The slinky brunette that has lured me across the room is ring-less. I'm assuming she's also date-less, or if not, she should be, because no way in hell would any decent man leave his girlfriend alone around the predators here. Predators like me.

It briefly occurs to me that I've never once thought of myself as a predator, and that maybe these ideas in my head are a sign that I need to get the fuck out of Dodge.

But I can't. For reasons I can't explain. Reasons that are primal and base and as out of my control as breathing.

As well as being ring-less, she's also drink-less, and so, as a waiter passes, I drop off my empty flute, and retrieve two fresh glasses.

When my prey turns casually in my direction, I'm ready.

I hold out a glass in her direction. "Champagne?"

Her grey eyes spark when they catch mine, sending a jolt straight to my dick. I'd know that look anywhere—she likes what she sees, and thank God, because now that I've seen her close up, I'm absolutely certain that I have to have her. Have to possess her. Have to do unspeakably dirty things to every inch of her body.

*Tighten those reins, boy. Get a hold of yourself.*

I almost do, but then she narrows her stare and twists her lip. It's the lip that does me in.

"How do I know you didn't put anything in it?" she asks, and

JesusfuckingChrist, she's got an English accent. I'm instantly hard.

Okay, semi-hard. I'm not twelve. I have some control.

"Well," I consider, "I have two drinks. You choose which one, and I'll drink the other."

She hesitates, suspicion vibrating from her body. Which is crazy—I'm a puppy.

Except I'm not a puppy. Not right now, not around her, and her distrust increases my interest in her tenfold.

"How about you drink from both of them? And then I'll choose one."

Whichever she chooses, she'll have her lips on the glass after mine. That's so hot.

Maybe I am only twelve.

With her eyes still caught in mine, I take a swallow from one flute and then from the other. "Now choose."

"I'll have this one," she says, claiming the glass I drank more from. "Thank you." Her skepticism relaxes slightly, but she's still wary. As she should be.

I'm surprised how much it arouses me.

Tipping it forward, I clink my flute to hers. "You've been surrounded all night."

"And?" She's polite enough not to sigh, but I can hear the weariness behind the single word.

I should leave her alone.

I can't. "I didn't like it."

She tilts her head, her expression both appalled and intrigued. "I don't really think it matters what you like."

"True, true." I give her the Chandler grin, the one that drops panties at the speed of light. "Thing is, I don't think you liked it either."

She crosses her arms over herself and leans her weight on one gorgeous hip. "So, since I didn't like a bunch of men trying to pick me up, you thought you'd come over and pick me up instead?"

"When you put it that way, I sound like an asshole."

"You said it, not me."

She seems truly put off, and I'm momentarily thrown off my game. Mostly because this isn't at all the game I usually play. Usually, *I'm* the target. There are too many already willing women to waste time working for one.

*Smile and say goodnight, Chandler.*

I take a swallow from my drink. The sweetness is so much more tolerable as I imagine licking it off her lips, and now that I've imagined it, there's no going back.

"How about I make it up to you?" I say, totally improvising. "When you're ready to go, I'll escort you out so no one bothers you. Once outside, you can totally tell me to take a hike."

She gives me the same expression she did before—the shocked and fascinated one—and this time I catch a hint of amusement as well. "You're really full of yourself, thinking I need you to help me get out of here."

An unexpected filthy, crass comment about filling her instead flutters on the tip of my tongue, but I push it away. *Play nice.* "I wasn't implying that at all. I'm just offering a service that could be mutually beneficial."

"How would that benefit you?"

"I'd get to be the guy seen walking out with the most beautiful woman in the room." *Yes!* Now my brain's on the right track.

She gives me an incredulous glare, but her icy demeanor has melted. "You American men are such charmers." She takes a sip from her drink, and when she licks her tongue over her bottom lip? Talk about melting. I'm so hot I'm a puddle of molten lava over this girl.

Somehow I manage to remain *charming.* "Oh," I mock groan, clutching my chest as though she's wounded my heart. "You've lumped me with the all the other 'American men.' That's a real low blow."

She laughs, and it's so adorable that I want to sink my teeth into the sound and bite, want to mark it and claim it as mine.

"Perhaps it was a little crueler than necessary," she says, then sobers quickly. "Let me ask you this—is being *seen* with me the only thing you're interested in?"

No, it's most definitely not at all. I'm also interested in fucking her. I'm interested in dragging her into a dark corner so I can feed her my cock. I'm interested in watching her ride me, her petite tits bouncing as she drives up and down the length of my shaft.

And now I *am* hard. So hard it hurts.

I don't answer. Which is an answer in itself.

Damn, I need to get out of here.

I catch sight of the crowd that had earlier surrounded her and use it as my excuse. "Your entourage seems to be returning. I'll let you attend to them." I will myself to turn and walk away, but my feet don't move, and before I know it, I'm leaning into her, so close I can smell her natural scent underneath her floral perfume.

"My offer stands if you want it," I say quietly. "Come and find me. I'll be here."

Shit. Now I've done it. If she has any sense, she'll tell me not to bother waiting around. It's my only hope.

But when I straighten, her eyes lock on mine, and I can't help but think she might be as twisted up over me as I am about her.

"Genevieve," she says, holding her hand out to me.

I barely manage to mask the shock that runs through me when my hand clasps around hers. "Chandler. Chandler Pierce."

Her brow rises in recognition, and for the first time in my life, I'm worried about my reputation. Usually, I wear my name like it's a designer brand. My name gets me things I like. Gets me out of speeding tickets and into the arms of pretty women.

But I've never cared who the pretty woman was—this time I do. This time, I want the pretty woman to be this one. I want *Genevieve*.

Her expression is unreadable, and I can't tell if I've just sealed the deal or if I've blown any chance I might have had.

Then she says, "It's been a pleasure, Mr. Pierce," and turns to greet the gentleman who has just arrived at her side, also carrying two flutes of champagne.

Though she clings to the one I gave her, her dismissal is clear. *Mr. Pierce*, she said. So cold and detached. So utterly unimpressed.

I take the cue and slip away. I should leave the event entirely, but I can't force myself to go. I told her I'd be here, and maybe it's because I really am a nice guy that I can't seem to bring myself to break my word.

Or maybe I just can't bear to let her go yet.

I mingle. Some woman I've fucked in the past drapes herself over my shoulder and introduces her friend who drapes herself over my other arm. *This* is my audience. I could take either of them home right now. Both of them.

But as they fawn, my focus is on Genevieve. I watch as she excuses herself from her admirers. My gaze follows her as she approaches a group of men. She taps one on the shoulder, one old enough to be her father. He puts a finger up, telling her to wait, and I bristle at the gesture because it's rude but also because it's familiar. Just like I didn't like the crowd that had surrounded her, I don't like what this man might be to her. I have no right to care. I've only just met her, and every interest I have in her is carnal. Yet I do care. Very much.

Which is why, when I see her heading toward me a few minutes later, I already know I'm about to say or do something I shouldn't.

Ignoring the women clinging to me, Genevieve looks me straight in the eye. "Does your offer still stand, Chandler? Because I'm ready to go now."

I don't hesitate even a beat. "Definitely," I say, shucking off the women as though they were a well-worn jacket. I slip my hand in Genevieve's. "Let's go, shall we?"

Told you I'd do something I shouldn't. Sorry, Hudson.

# On behalf of 1001 Dark Nights,

Liz Berry and M.J. Rose would like to thank ~

Steve Berry
Doug Scofield
Kim Guidroz
Jillian Stein
InkSlinger PR
Dan Slater
Asha Hossain
Chris Graham
Pamela Jamison
Jessica Johns
Dylan Stockton
Richard Blake
BookTrib After Dark
The Dinner Party Show
and Simon Lipskar

Printed in Great Britain
by Amazon